Brighton Island

Holly Copella

To Lori Beltz

ACKNOWLEDGMENTS

Copella Books: First Paperback Edition 2018
Printed by CreateSpace, An Amazon.com Company
Cover Artist: Daniela Owergoor
Dani-owergoor.deviantart.com

PUBLISHER'S NOTE

Chapter One

Brighton Island was a private, secluded island in the Atlantic Ocean just off the coast of Florida. Its white, sandy beach contained an impressive boathouse with a sturdy dock. The beach circled nearly the entire island, while the center was mostly covered in woods. Barely visible from the beach, the island mansion was a one-hundred yard trek up a small roadway. The mansion consisted of the main building and a north and south wing. One wing was in disrepair to the point of creepy, while the other wing was undergoing major renovations.

The main house had been painstakingly restored to its original beauty and grandeur. Made almost entirely of stone, the mansion had an almost medieval appeal. Tall, broad windows covered both stories and the second floor had several bedrooms with sturdy balconies. Despite darkness setting in, there were few lights on within the mansion for early evening.

The elegant, natural wood study had a wall of windows along the back, allowing for natural light and a beautiful view of the garden. An oversized, mahogany desk was the showpiece of the room. There were bookcases along the wall on either side of the stone fireplace. On the opposite side of the room was a credenza containing several bottles of alcohol and a large gun case with shotguns, rifles, and handguns.

A man in his mid-fifties, Major Dexter Hyland, unlocked the gun cabinet. Hyland, as he preferred to be called, stood a tick over six foot and was built moderately muscular and solid. Despite living in a multi-million dollar mansion, he looked as if he'd be more at home at the gun range. His head was as clean-shaven as his face, giving him an intimidating appearance. With his military background, the major *was* as intimidating as he looked.

An impeccably dressed butler in his early fifties entered the study and eyed his employer as he rummaged through the assortment of handguns. Ellis was shorter than average and had a lean, non-impressive build. His brown hair was short and professional to match his meticulously clean-shaven face. He had a docile, sweet appearance rarely seen outside a Muppet. His black butler's uniform was made from the finest threads and pressed to near perfection. Ellis had the appearance of the perfect butler. Refined, well-bred, and well-mannered.

"Sir, your niece called," Ellis announced with little emotion. "She'll be here in the morning."

Hyland looked at Ellis sharply with some surprise. "Jacklyn?" he practically gasped then immediately shook his head. "No, you need to tell her not to come. This isn't a good time."

Ellis watched Hyland insert a loaded magazine into a semiautomatic pistol from the cabinet. He raised a curious brow.

"Is something wrong, sir?"

Hyland cocked the weapon. "Nothing a little violence won't solve," he replied with a mocking grin.

As Hyland left the room, Ellis eyed the open gun cabinet.

Chapter Two

The stone dungeon was a maze of corridors and cells dimly lit by electric torches with real torches sporadically placed, giving it an authentic feel. Despite the authenticity of the dungeon, it wasn't nearly as damp and drafty as one would suspect. Hyland carried his gun partially concealed alongside his thigh while looking around the dimly lit, stone corridor.

"I know you're down here," Hyland announced while concealing his devious grin as well as the gun. "Come on out, and we'll talk."

Hyland listened a moment then looked around. It was almost as if he could hear someone nearby, yet the dungeon appeared quiet. A faint echoing sound could be heard, but it was nearly impossible to tell from which direction or corridor it came. He raised the gun in front of him, holding it in a professionally trained manner, and then cautiously entered one of the connecting corridors. For a brief moment, the dungeon was eerily silent. A gunshot rang out, breaking the silence, and echoed throughout the dungeon.

§

Morning. The mansion kitchen contained modern and antique appliances for functionality and eye appeal, although the antique counterparts were rarely used. The massive island counter could easily seat six staff on the outer side and still leave enough room on the inner side for the cook to perform his duties for a large party. A large, burly cook in his late twenties sat at the counter huddled over a cup of coffee and appeared exhausted. Regan had dark nearly black, wild curly hair and neatly trimmed facial hair that loosely resembled a beard. Ellis entered the kitchen and approached the island counter with the same look of exhaustion.

"Any luck?" Ellis asked his weary counterpart.

Regan shook his head while attempting to keep his eyes open as his temple rested on his fist. "None, dude," he muttered. "We've been up all night looking for him. He's totally vanished."

A casually dressed woman in her late twenties entered the kitchen from the main entrance. She looked equally worn and collapsed at the table. Ellis poured a cup of coffee and placed it on the table in front of the woman. She groaned and accepted the coffee.

"I certainly hope we weren't up searching half the night just to discover he'd taken the boat to the mainland," Leanne muttered.

"No, the yacht is still docked in the boathouse," Ellis assured her.

Leanne was the attractive, live-in maid. Her long, blonde hair was pulled back into a ponytail, as custom while she worked. She had an attention-grabbing figure, although she tended to hide it beneath a pair of casual jeans and an oversized shirt. Given her job, her attire was casual and comfortable.

Leanne sipped her coffee then shook her head. "I don't know where he could be then," she announced. "Between the three of us, we must have searched the entire mansion. The horses are in the pasture, and none of the four wheelers are missing, so if he ventured out into the woods, he went on foot."

"I doubt the major went hiking," Ellis remarked.

"Maybe we should, like, check the dungeon and the north wing," Regan suggested.

"Why would he go either of those places?" Leanne practically demanded while glaring at the cook. "They're both dark, dirty rattraps."

The sound of a distant helicopter broke the usually peaceful island paradise. All three perked up and listened to the sound as it grew louder and closer.

"What's that?" Regan asked with confusion.

"Sounds like a helicopter," Ellis remarked, although obviously baffled by the possibility.

Chapter Three

The top-of-the-line, brand-new, six-passenger helicopter shut down on the beach not far from the dock and the path to the mansion. Apparently, someone had gotten a new toy. The pilot in his late twenties was a neatly dressed man with an air of wealth about him as well as a childish appeal. Simon climbed out of the pilot's seat, looked at the mansion in the near distance, and nodded his approval while grinning like a schoolboy.

"Yeah, I need to get me one of those," Simon announced and chuckled.

Simon was a decent looking man in his own rights. His lanky build and neatly trimmed hair went well with his expensive, stylish clothing. A young woman in her mid-twenties got out of the co-pilot's seat and looked at the mansion in the distance as well. Jacklyn Hyland laughed then glanced at her unusual friend.

"For about twenty million, you can have one," she teased.

Jacklyn wore her long, dark hair up in a simple ponytail and dressed rather plain alongside the fashionably dressed man. Jacklyn was built athletic with enough cleavage and curves to gain plenty of male attention. Simon removed their duffel bags from the helicopter, refusing to let her carry her own bag, and followed her to the well-groomed path.

"When my cousins would visit, we'd play all day in the dungeon, exploring and looking for pirates' treasure," Jacklyn informed him as she relived her childhood with fondness.

"The dungeon?" Simon announced while grinning. "That sounds like fun. When I was a boy, we'd search for Pharaoh's treasure in our pyramid tent." He chuckled nervously. "Growing up with professors as parents makes for a serious childhood."

"I wouldn't exactly call you serious," Jacklyn teased. "But I wasn't kidding. Supposedly there was actual pirates' treasure in the dungeon caverns."

"You'll have to tell me more about that later while we're exploring," he remarked then grinned. "I'm actually curious to hear how this hard-core uncle of yours ended up here, and why you call him Uncle Hyland rather than Uncle Dexter?"

"Well, he hates the name Dexter and will probably punch you if you call him that. As for his story. My uncle, the major, was devoted to the military until he met and fell in love with Lady Mara Brighton," she announced with a romantic sigh. "He walked away from sixteen years in the service to marry her. The island and mansion were given to Aunt Mara on her eighteenth birthday." She eyed Simon and held back her laugh. "It took twelve years for her to finally meet someone crazy enough to live here with her."

"So how did you end up living here?" Simon asked while looking around.

"My aunt and uncle took me in after my parents died when I was fifteen," she informed him. "Unfortunately, Aunt Mara died two years later. To fulfill her wishes, my uncle spent millions remodeling the place the way she always dreamed it would be." She hid her humored grin. "The construction workers and his architect have been living here the last two years, and they're still only about half-finished with the south wing."

Ellis appeared on the path in a luxury golf cart. Simon was moderately surprised to see the golf cart mysteriously appear, but he seemed happy that he wouldn't have to tote the bags all the way up to the mansion.

Ellis stared at her with surprise. "Ms. Hyland, didn't you get my message?" he asked while tilting his head. "Your uncle asked to postpone your visit. Now isn't a good time."

"I haven't checked my messages," she informed him then took the bags from Simon and tossed them into the back of the golf cart. "I'm avoiding Uncle Harry. I think he's sniffing out some money."

"Your Uncle Harry sounds like fun," Simon muttered.

Ellis watched as they climbed into the back of the cart behind him and appeared ready to protest. He was, essentially, asking her to leave. Jacklyn eyed the look she received from the butler then smiled and held back her laugh.

"Come now, Ellis," she announced with humor and leaned back in the seat. "Do you actually think my uncle would expect me to just pick up and leave? We're already here."

Ellis drew a deep breath, possibly knowing it was his ass for not pressing the issue. He reluctantly turned the cart around on the beach in order to make the journey back to the mansion with the newly arrived guests.

Chapter Four

Ellis carried their bags into the foyer and set them down just inside the doorway. There were four steps down to the grand hallway with restored hardwood floor leading all the way back to the kitchen. The marble and brass grand staircase was broad, spiraled slightly, and seemed to stretch to heaven. Jacklyn and Simon followed Ellis inside. Simon immediately marveled at the foyer, grand hallway, and massive staircase.

"I'm sorry we're shorthanded this morning," Ellis announced. "Leanne is helping with another matter. Your *friend* can have the room across the hall from you. If you'd kindly show yourselves to your rooms--"

They heard arguing male voices as two men walked along the hallway heading toward them from the south wing corridor. Brandon was a handsome man in his early thirties with short black hair and a clean-shaven face. He was close to six feet tall with an athletic build, although not incredibly muscular. Rick, on the other hand, was a muscular man in his mid-thirties. He had short, slightly spiky, dirty blonde hair and ruggedly handsome features. He stood a few inches taller than Brandon and had a more commanding presence. Both men saw Ellis and nearly pounced on him, dragging him into their little spat.

"Ellis, where the hell is Hyland?" Rick demanded and didn't even notice Jacklyn and Simon.

"The village idiot here is attempting to dig a tunnel one hundred yards from the south wing," Brandon announced in a callous tone with irritation.

Ellis stared at him with surprise. "One hundred yards from the south wing?" he remarked and appeared bewildered. "That's under the cemetery."

"That's what I've been telling him," Brandon announced while gesturing with his hands.

"And I'm telling you, we're nowhere near the cemetery," Rick launched back while maintaining his calm demeanor.

"Stop digging before a casket falls on your head," Ellis informed Rick then glared at Brandon. "And you work on that charming personality of yours."

"Nicely handled, Ellis," Jacklyn teased.

Both men were suddenly aware of Jacklyn and Simon standing within the foyer.

Rick took a quick step toward them and grinned in what was meant to be a charming manner. "Sorry about the yelling," he announced. "I hope we didn't offend you, Miss--?"

"Put your charm back in your pants," Brandon scoffed while glaring at Rick. "That's Hyland's niece."

"Mind your manners, Brandon," Ellis remarked then turned his attention to Jacklyn. "This is Rick, the construction supervisor, and Brandon, your uncle's architect."

"We've been introduced," Brandon replied.

"I don't think so," Jacklyn corrected while studying him. She was positive she would have remembered meeting the handsome architect.

"Sure we have," Brandon announced then smiled teasingly. "Your uncle pointed you out across the room and told me what he'd do to me if I so much as looked at you. I remember the introduction quite clear."

"Sounds like my uncle," she announced and held back her laugh. She then glanced at Simon and nodded to the stairs. "Let's get settled into our rooms."

Jacklyn and Simon approached the massive staircase and headed up them for the second floor.

Ellis placed his hands on his temples and glared at both men. "Can you two please go away now?"

Regan poked his head into the hallway from the kitchen down the hall. "Hey, dudes," he called out. "Fresh coffee and pastries being served this way!"

Both men eagerly hurried down the hall to join Regan. Ellis smiled his appreciation to the happy-go-lucky cook.

Chapter Five

A little while later, Simon sat at the island counter with a plate of sandwiches before him while Regan stood on the other side and watched him eat. Jacklyn leaned on the counter and made a face while marveling at the quantities of food her friend was able to consume considering his lean frame.

"These are the best sandwiches I've ever had," Simon announced. "How's that possible?"

"They're made with love, man," Regan announced. "Never forget the love."

Jacklyn finally looked at Regan and appeared curious. "So where is Uncle Hyland?"

"Didn't Ellis tell you?" Regan asked with surprise while staring at her as his eyes widened dramatically. "We can't find him. He just sort of vanished."

Jacklyn straightened and stared at him with horror. "What do you mean he vanished?"

"We looked for him all night," Regan replied. "He was here, and then he was gone. We haven't looked in the old wing or the dungeon yet."

"We'll check the north wing then the dungeon," Jacklyn announced and eyed Simon, who proceeded to stuff another sandwich into his mouth then grabbed one for the road.

"After I serve lunch, I'll help," Regan informed her.

"Okay, we'll start in the north wing then meet up with you in the torture chamber," Jacklyn replied.

Regan cringed and fidgeted. "Dude, why there?"

§

Jacklyn and Simon entered the north wing ballroom.

The north wing was under construction, although most of the wing had yet to be touched with renovations. The massive gathering room had marble floors, tall windows covered with boards, and sheet-covered antiques. The windows contained stained glass along the top half. At one time, it would have been a showcase for gatherings. Despite being dirty and dimly lit, Simon looked around with complete awe.

"I can almost hear the orchestra." Simon turned to Jacklyn, grinned charmingly, and extended his hand. "May I have this dance, my lady?"

"I'd be honored."

Simon took Jacklyn into his arms, and they glided across the dusty, marble floor to the non-existent music. As they waltzed across the room, he released her and uncovered the grand piano. He lovingly ran his hands along the keys.

"Do you have any idea how old this piano is?" Simon practically gasped.

"Probably as old as the mansion."

Simon tapped on the keys and grimaced. "And terribly out of key." His enthusiastic smile returned. "Would your uncle mind if I camped out here a few nights?" he asked. "I want to get a feel for the old girl."

Jacklyn laughed and shook her head. "You're almost too weird for words."

"Yeah, but you love me anyway," he remarked then looked around. "Judging by the dust on the floor, we're the only ones who've been here in years. There's no way your uncle was through here."

"You're right," she replied. "Let's try the dungeon."

Chapter Six

The dungeon corridor was damp, dingy, and dimly lit. Jacklyn lit several real torches between the electric ones for added light as they walked along the stone corridor. Simon continued to look around in complete amazement.

"It must have been something having this place as your playground," Simon announced. "I would have been in my glory growing up here."

"I had a sleepover for my sixteenth birthday," she informed him. "I insisted we were going to sleep in the dungeon."

Simon eyed her and beamed with enthusiasm. "That sounds awesome."

"We lasted thirty-five minutes before running upstairs screaming," she announced while grinning.

Jacklyn and Simon entered the torture chamber. Despite the lit torches, the room remained dingy and moderately dirty. The remnants of old torture devices were still mostly intact and spread sporadically around the room. There was an old wooden stretching rack, iron maiden, and various other torture devices meant to maim. Simon turned the wheel on the stretching rack. Nothing happened. He frowned with disappointment.

"Obviously, everything has been disabled," she informed him while holding back her laugh.

"So disrespectful," he muttered.

Simon cast himself onto the stretching rack and attempted to put his wrists into the rusted shackles. They didn't close.

"And that would be why things are disabled," she teased while mocking him.

Simon sat up on the rack and looked around while nodding his approval. "This has got to be the creepiest place I've ever visited in my life." He then looked at her as his eyes lit up with morbid enthusiasm. "Let's have that sleepover. We can tell ghost stories and roast marshmallows over the hot coals."

They heard low, ghostly moans echoing off the walls. Both looked around, unable to tell from where the sounds were coming. The moans were distorted and frightening. Simon jumped off the rack and grabbed Jacklyn's arm.

"And moving on--"

Simon pushed Jacklyn to the open door. They nearly collided with Regan and Brandon. Simon and Regan cried out after having nearly collided.

"Dude," Regan screamed. "Are you trying to give me a heart attack?"

"Oh, what we heard was just voices echoing through the vents," Jacklyn announced and managed a soft, nervous laugh.

"Brandon offered to help look for Hyland," Regan informed them.

"I'm pretty sure you begged me to come along," Brandon announced casually.

Regan glared at Brandon. "Dude, begged is a strong word. More like threatened to cut off the pastry supply line."

Chapter Seven

Brandon, Jacklyn, Regan, and Simon walked along the dungeon corridor. There was an unusual breeze blowing past them, catching their attention.

"What's causing that breeze?" Simon asked while looking around.

"There's an old underground cavern," Jacklyn informed him then made a face. "It's dark and filled with water. Sort of like an underground pond. A little too creepy for my taste."

Brandon stood aside and extended his hand down the corridor while eyeing Jacklyn. "Since you know the way, lead on."

"I can't imagine why he'd go there or even be down here in the first place," Jacklyn remarked.

Brandon chuckled. "Scared?"

She groaned with annoyance and walked past him. They walked for several minutes before reaching an archway, similar to every other archway within the dungeon. The old, thick door was now open. All four stood on the stone landing above what appeared to be an underground dock. The narrow stone steps were steep, contained no railing, and led down to the water-filled cavern nearly two stories below. An old, half-sunken boat was attached to the dock by a rotted rope. A narrow, water-filled tunnel could be seen to the left.

Regan remained clinging to the archway and peered down to the dark water below. Brandon shined his flashlight onto the steep steps as he proceeded down them. Jacklyn and Simon were reluctant to follow. The steep, open steps unnerved Jacklyn even when she was an adventurous young teenager. The thought alone made her moderately dizzy. She also hated standing on the landing just on the other side of the archway since there was no railing there either. It seemed like a steep drop, even though it wasn't all that steep.

"Dude, are you sure you want to do that?" Regan asked as his eyes widened with concern while he clung to the security of the archway.

Brandon ignored him and continued to the bottom. He shined his light into the dark water then to the tunnel. The tunnel was more than halfway filled with water. Had Jacklyn not pointed it out, the tunnel would easily go unnoticed.

"He's not here," Regan insisted while seeming tense, afraid to move onto the questionable landing. "Can we go now?"

Brandon returned up the steps and joined the others. Regan was quick to hurry back into the dungeon corridor. Jacklyn was quick to follow. All four walked along one of many dimly lit dungeon corridors. They'd been walking for several minutes in what seemed like an endless maze of stone corridors lined with old cells. Simon walked alongside Jacklyn and looked around the corridor with some uncertainty.

"How do you know we're not just going in circles?" Simon finally asked.

"There are numbers on the cells," Brandon answered his question.

Regan eyed Brandon, seeming surprised by his knowledge of the rarely traveled dungeon. "Come down here a lot?" he asked with sarcasm in his tone.

"I got lost down here once," he casually replied. "You learn a lot when you're hopelessly lost."

Simon kicked something on the floor. They heard a tiny, metallic clank as the object rolled across the floor. Brandon picked up a bullet casing and stared at it with a curious look.

"What is it?" Jacklyn asked.

"A bullet casing from a handgun," Brandon replied then sniffed it. "It smells fresh."

Brandon handed it to Jacklyn then shined the flashlight along the walls. They saw a fresh chip in the stone wall. He followed the corridor, stopped, and shined his light at a wet spot on the floor. He crouched down and dabbed the dark spot with his index finger.

Jacklyn hurried to join him. "What did you find?"

"Blood--" Brandon immediately shined his light around the corridor.

"Someone got shot down here?" Regan cried out, his voice echoing along the corridors.

Brandon discovered a small trail of blood droplets and immediately followed them. The others hurried after him. The droplets led into a nearby cell. He stopped before the closed cell door and shined his light into it. They saw a covered mass in the back. Brandon pulled open the unlocked door and hurried inside with Jacklyn directly behind him. He pulled back the old blanket to reveal a motionless Hyland.

"Uncle Hyland!"

Brandon kneeled alongside him and visually examined him. "He's alive, but someone gave him one hell of a knock on the head." He nudged the unconscious man. "Hyland, can you hear me?" When he didn't respond, he nudged him a little harder.

Hyland groaned and attempted to open his eyes. "Who the hell is hitting me?"

Chapter Eight

Hyland held ice to a bump and laceration on his forehead while Jacklyn and Simon sat beside him at the kitchen table. Regan hurried toward them with a first aid kit as Ellis entered the kitchen.

"What happened?" Ellis demanded.

"Dude, someone, like, brained him and left him in a dungeon cell," Regan announced and joined them at the table with the first aid kit.

Ellis pulled the ice from Hyland's head to reveal the bleeding gash. "You need to go to the emergency room," he insisted.

"No hospitals," Hyland growled.

"You need stitches," Ellis snapped back.

"Fine, call a doctor, but I'm not going to any hospital," Hyland launched in anger.

The butler muttered something and approached the kitchen phone. He immediately contacted the mainland.

"Ellis will make a fine, nagging wife one day," Hyland retorted.

"He's fine," Brandon announced and stood. "You know where to find me if you need me."

As Brandon left, Hyland glanced at Simon several times then back at Jacklyn. "Who's that guy?"

"That's my friend, Simon," she informed him. "I told you about him the last time we spoke."

"Needs a little meat on his bones," Hyland muttered then cast a look at Regan. "Regan, take care of that."

"Already on it, boss dude."

Jacklyn studied her uncle's condition and shook her head. "Who'd do this?"

"A boatload of construction workers, a disgruntled architect, half the Russian Navy," Hyland announced then considered his comment. "All of Afghanistan."

"Be serious," Jacklyn scolded.

"Okay, maybe not *all* of Afghanistan," he muttered.

Ellis looked at them from across the kitchen. "Perhaps you'd like to tell her why you took a gun from the cabinet on your little nature walk."

"I don't remember that," Hyland snapped then demandingly glared at Ellis, "and I can't imagine why you'd tell her if I had."

Ellis hung up the phone. "The doctor is on his way," he announced. "I'll meet him at the dock." He then left the kitchen through the back door.

"You're being a little hard on Ellis," Jacklyn informed him.

"He's turning into my mother," Hyland muttered.

Jacklyn drew a deep breath and looked at her friend. "Simon, why don't you go with Ellis," she suggested. "I'll stay with my uncle."

Simon nodded and left the kitchen through the outer door. Regan sheepishly followed as if anticipating something was about to unfold. Jacklyn glared at Hyland as he looked at the blood on the ice pack.

"What is your problem?" Jacklyn suddenly demanded in an angry tone.

Hyland looked at her with surprise. "Why are you yelling at me? Can't you see I'm bleeding?"

"Ellis spends the entire night looking for you, and all you can do is insult him and snarl at everyone," she launched with hostility.

Hyland stared at her seemingly speechless then suddenly smiled and laughed softly. "Well, aren't you the little spitfire today."

"Yeah, I get it from you," she snapped. "I want to know what's going on."

"Someone's trying to scare me away."

"Who in their right mind would think they could scare you?" she demanded, not believing a word he said. "Children look under their beds for Major Dexter Hyland."

"Of course I can't be scared away; thus the shock and awe on my head," he boldly announced. "I heard someone playing around in the dungeon, so I went to investigate."

"With a loaded gun?"

He casually shrugged. "What can I say? I play rough." He eyed her sharply and raised an arrogant brow. "Now, tell me about this Simon fellow and why I shouldn't hate him."

"Stop changing the subject."

Chapter Nine

Morning. The large conservatory within the west wing was partially renovated and contained new windows stretching from the floor to the ceiling, new hardwood floor, and a cathedral ceiling. Scaffolding was still erected where the workers were restoring the sculpted trim around the ceiling and windows. Three construction workers appeared to be on an endless coffee break. Norman, Anderson, and Cooper stood around the table containing the coffeepot and homemade pastries while laughing at something one of the men had said.

Jacklyn and Simon entered the conservatory and looked around in silent awe. The room had come a long way since her last visit just a few weeks earlier. Jacklyn allowed her eyes to fall upon the three construction workers. Apart from the three men, the room was abandoned. She'd seen most of the construction crew before but usually avoided the areas under construction as a general rule. The men were always busy, and their equipment made a lot of noise. The three were tall, well-built men in their late thirties. They seemed to share the same muscular build, short hair, and two days' worth of facial stubble. Jacklyn and Simon approached the three workers, who immediately noticed her and smiled their silent approval.

"Well, good morning," Anderson announced a little too eagerly.

As the worker gave Jacklyn a stealthy once over, Simon frowned in disapproval. Although she didn't seem to mind the man's harmless flirting, she wasted little time getting to the point of her visit.

"I'm looking for Rick," she informed the three, slacking men.

"He's over there," Cooper replied while nodding in the direction of the table.

Jacklyn was about to correct the man since she knew they were the only three workers in the room, but when she looked in the direction he'd indicated, she saw Rick by the table. Rick studied his blueprints and didn't pay much attention to the lazy workers. He hadn't even noticed Jacklyn and Simon within the room. Jacklyn and Simon were slightly baffled by the foreman's sudden reappearing act. Jacklyn nudged Simon. They crossed the room and approached Rick at his portable drafting table. He looked up from his blueprints, saw them, and immediately beamed with delight.

"Miss Hyland, I presume," he teased.

For the muscly construction worker type, he was rather pleasant and playful. Being ruggedly handsome was an added bonus. Jacklyn couldn't deny he was quite attractive. Placed alongside Simon; Simon looked almost scrawny in comparison.

"I expected to see more workers," Jacklyn replied while looking around. "My uncle made it sound like there were a dozen or more living in the mansion."

"There usually are. The others went to the mainland for the weekend," he replied cheerfully. "We work with a skeleton crew on the weekends. It's usually just the four of us." A sly smile crossed his face. "You know the ambitious ones who enjoy overtime pay." He then motioned her to follow him. "You're going to love what we found this morning."

Jacklyn and Simon appeared curious and followed Rick across the room. He pushed a panel alongside the fireplace. The wall opened to reveal a secret passageway. Simon and Jacklyn stared at the narrow opening and beamed with enthusiasm.

"Oh, wow," Jacklyn gasped.

"We haven't checked it out yet," Rick informed her while grinning.

"I think we're about to go exploring," Simon announced with a chuckle.

"I'll get a flashlight," Jacklyn practically cried out.

Rick grinned and handed her one. She flashed a smile, grabbed the flashlight, and entered the narrow opening.

"Are you sure you don't want me to lead?" Simon asked, but there was no stopping Jacklyn while she was pursuing an adventure.

Chapter Ten

Jacklyn led Simon and Rick through the narrow, stone passageway. She grimaced while removing thick cobwebs collecting on her face. She just hoped the spiders had vacated the area. The thought of spiders crawling across her body gave her the willies.

"Gross," she whined while pulling the webs from her face and spitting some out.

"Told you I should lead," Simon remarked.

"We're at the end," she informed them then felt the wall before her.

Jacklyn pulled a lever that opened a panel revealing a secret parlor. All three stepped into the dimly lit sitting room within the south wing. The heavy, dirty curtains were drawn over a set of large windows, and the dusty furniture remained uncovered possibly for decades. Despite its age and neglect, the furniture was in good shape, although a tacky burgundy color. There was an open doorway leading into what was possibly a bedroom. The remaining walls were painted the same tacky burgundy color as the furniture. The hardwood floors were dull with a thick layer of dust, revealing only their footprints.

The gaudy room almost reminded Jacklyn of something one might find in an old-fashioned whorehouse. All three looked around with amazement. There was no telling how long the room had gone unnoticed. Their amazement turned to possible concern.

"Uh, does anyone else notice something wrong here?" Jacklyn announced.

"Yeah, no exit doors," Simon muttered. "Maybe there's an exit in the next room."

All three entered the attached bedroom. The hidden bedroom was much smaller than most of the main house bedrooms. It contained antique furniture and expensive, dust coated paintings. Considering nothing had been covered, it was safe to assume no one knew about the hidden rooms. They discovered another wall containing large windows and an attached bathroom, but there were still no exit doors, which meant the only way in and out of the hidden rooms was through the secret passageway. It was an amazing discovery.

Simon approached the bathroom doorway and peered inside. His expression immediately dropped as horror crossed his face.

"Jacklyn?" Simon gasped then he started to panic. "Jacklyn!"

Jacklyn and Rick joined him in the bathroom doorway and immediately saw what frightened him. Within the old-fashioned, white tiled bathroom, they saw a severely decayed, possibly naked woman within the empty, bloodstained, claw-foot tub. Jacklyn nervously approached the tub containing the woman who must have been rotting within it for years. Her body was partially shriveled with dark, wrinkled skin hanging from her frame. Her eyes had rotted away entirely along with most of her muscle, which just left her skin hanging over her bones. Her long, golden blonde hair was the only creepy reminder that she had once been alive. Had she been taking a bath in the strange, secret room when she died?

Jacklyn could clearly tell the dead woman had been naked at the time. Her eyes then strayed to the bloodstain surrounding the bottom of the tub, almost as if there had been no water in the tub at the time of her death. Jacklyn then noticed a large opening in the woman's neck. It didn't look like any wound she'd ever seen before. It almost looked chewed. There was a matching opening in the dead woman's abdomen.

Jacklyn took a step closer to study the strange wounds when the decayed body moved. Jacklyn jumped back and let out a horrified gasp as the woman's body writhed within the tub. Rick and Simon bolted back through the doorway and peered into the bathroom from a distance. As the woman's body moved within the tub, Jacklyn debated making a run for it, but she couldn't convince her feet to move.

Dozens of rats suddenly scurried out from inside the dead woman's body cavity, ran up her decayed leg, and dropped to the floor before finding their own exit from the bathroom. Jacklyn cried out and nearly ran into Simon and Rick. Rick covered his mouth and heaved several times at the sight of the rats scurrying out of the decayed body.

Chapter Eleven

An hour later, Jacklyn stood near the doorway to the secret bedroom with Hyland, who held her while police and paramedics milled about the mysterious, hidden room. Rick leaned against the wall near a newly found secret entrance from the hallway. The paramedics brought out the stretcher with the black body bag containing the dead woman. Simon nervously stood near the open curtains, which allowed sunlight to flood into the once dark room. Detective Reed from the mainland police department approached them. The detective was possibly in his early fifties and looked more like a gritty city cop. He was slightly overweight, his clothes were shabby and more than a little wrinkled, and he looked as if he hadn't slept or shaved in days.

"No one knows who she was?" Detective Reed asked while rubbing his brow with his pen.

Everyone shook their heads.

"How long do you suppose she was there?" Hyland asked while clinging to Jacklyn.

"I'm guessing she'd been dead at least five years," Detective Reed informed him. "I've never seen this sort of decomposition. If the rats hadn't gotten to her, I'd say she was pretty well-preserved being locked away in this room. We'll have a better idea after the autopsy."

"Detective, where are her clothes?" Jacklyn asked while pulling away from her uncle. "I would assume she had some when she came into this room."

"Why would her killer take her clothes?" Simon asked with a curious look.

"We don't know that she was murdered," Detective Reed insisted.

"If she wasn't murdered," Jacklyn announced, "then her clothes should be in either the parlor or the bedroom. Someone obviously took her clothes, so she wasn't alone when she died, which must mean she was murdered."

Detective Reed stared at Jacklyn a moment and conceded. "Yes, it's possible she was murdered," he reluctantly informed her. "I haven't ruled out foul play."

§

Later that evening, Simon entered the hidden parlor beneath the yellow police line from the newly opened hall entrance. He stepped into the bedroom, looked around, and then sat on the bed and shut his eyes.

"I'm back, and I'm ready to listen," he announced to no one in particular.

There were flashes of a dagger, a woman's horrified face, and blood spattering from the tub. A woman's chilling scream filled the room.

Simon jerked while pinching his eyes shut. "You need to tell me who did this."

There were flashes of a costume party, people having a good time, and many masks. Music played and people danced. The images raced in fast forward. The horrifying images within the bathroom once again flashed.

Simon jerked and clutched his knees. "No, you're blocking. He can't hurt you anymore," he announced without opening his eyes. "Tell me who did this to you."

There were images of a man in a black, western-style undertaker costume in the ballroom surrounded by others in costume. His image was seen again with a dagger. There was a woman's chilling scream.

Simon finally gasped and opened his eyes. He cried out while holding his head as if in agony. The woman's screams continued to echo nearly shattering his eardrums. Simon clutched his head and leaped off the bed.

"Stop! Stop! It's too much!"

The sound of glass shattering came from the bathroom, alarming him. Simon stumbled into the open doorway where he stood while holding his head. The shattered mirror was scattered across the floor and contained blood spatters. Blood began filling the tub, sink, and toilet.

Simon shook his head. "No! Stop!"

The blood spilled out over the claw-foot tub and onto the white tiled floor. Bloody female footprints appeared on the floor and approached him.

"Stop! Stop," he screamed in terror while staring at the approaching bloody footprints.

A shadow loomed over him from behind, but he didn't notice.

"What are you doing?" came a male voice.

Simon cried out with surprise then spun around to see Brandon standing behind him. He quickly turned back toward the bathroom then saw the clean floor with the mirror intact and appeared stunned. He whirled back around to face Brandon and was unable to speak while rubbing his temples.

"The police said not to disturb the crime scene," Brandon reminded him.

"Yeah, I know. I had a little too much to drink and needed to see it again," Simon informed him while fumbling over his words as he continued to rub his temples. "Don't tell Jacklyn I'd been drinking. She'd be very disappointed in me."

Brandon eyed him suspiciously and nodded. "Yeah, no problem. Just sleep it off, okay?"

Simon fidgeted nervously although he could barely look at Brandon. "Yeah, I will. Thanks, man."

Brandon nodded and returned to the hallway through the open, secret hallway entrance. Simon again looked at the clean bathroom then pinched his eyes shut and groaned while ramming his fingertips into his temples.

"Get out of my head," he muttered. "Get out of my head!"

Chapter Twelve

That evening, Jacklyn, Hyland, Ellis, and Regan sat at the kitchen table enjoying coffee and cookies. The mood appeared to have lightened since their earlier, grisly find. Regan's storytelling was the highlight of their evening.

"Then in walks Lady Brighton, dressed to the hilt as Queen Mary--" Regan announced.

"Queen Elizabeth," Ellis corrected.

Regan glared at the butler and appeared moderately offended. "Who's telling this story, dude?" He looked back at the others and grinned. "She asks why there's no Merlot." His eyes widened dramatically. "What was I supposed to say? That her brother was doing one of the caterers in the wine cellar? So she drags me to the wine cellar, and there's her brother, bare bottomed, with a caterer bent over a case of Merlot." His look turned serious. "She calmly shuts the door, turns with this serious look on her face, and says, 'that vintage leaves something to be desired'."

Everyone at the table laughed.

Hyland shook his head while chuckling. "All night, she just kept saying, 'Harry is bad'."

"At least we know where Tara and Derek get their party groove," Jacklyn teased.

"That's a tasteful way of putting it," Ellis muttered as he approached the main counter.

Hyland eyed Ellis with a slightly surprised look then hid his humored grin. Ellis removed the coffeepot, returned to the table, and refilled all four mugs.

Hyland watched the butler with a curious look then felt compelled to change the subject. "What could you tell the police from five years ago?"

"From the party in question nearly five years ago, there were dozens of temporary wait staff and a lot of guests brought dates," he insisted, "but no one was reported missing."

"Maybe we should ask Uncle Harry when he gets here," Regan remarked and withheld his laugh. "I'll bet he remembers most of the female guests."

There was an awkward silence around the table.

"Harry is coming?" Hyland suddenly groused then eyed the butler. "Is there something you forgot to mention, Ellis?"

"No, I didn't forget to mention anything," Ellis casually replied. "I wasn't planning to tell you until they showed up."

"It'll be fine, Uncle Hyland," Jacklyn reassured him while placing a hand on his lower arm.

His look turned hateful. "Need I remind you that, although he felt it unnecessary to show up for his own sister's funeral, he had no trouble visiting her deathbed to ask for money," Hyland snarled while sitting back in his chair. "He blew through his entire inheritance on parties, booze, and expensive women then had the nerve to ask me for money, because, as he put it, 'it technically belonged to him anyway'." His lips twisted into a sneer. "I wanted to punch him in the face."

"If I recall correctly," Ellis remarked, "you did punch him in the face."

Brandon entered the kitchen without comment and opened the refrigerator.

Regan saw him and immediately became alert. "Stay out of the cream puffs, man."

Brandon straightened from the refrigerator while biting into a cream puff then gave an innocent look. "What? These?" he announced with a mouthful of pastry. "Oh, I'm sorry."

"Dude! Not cool," he cried out then looked at Jacklyn. "That's my midnight pastry thief. Took me months to catch him."

Jacklyn laughed then glanced at Brandon across the kitchen as he finished his cream puff. "Care to join us, Brandon?"

Brandon hesitated while staring at her then indicated her uncle alongside her with a slight nod. "See that icy look in your uncle's eyes?" he asked. "Translated, that look says, 'do and die, cream puff'."

Hyland chuckled at the comment.

Jacklyn pushed out the chair alongside her to her right. "I'll protect you from my big, bad uncle."

Brandon uncertainly rounded the table. Brandon and Hyland continued to watch each other as he sat. Their eyes locked over Jacklyn between them.

Hyland cried out and glared at his niece. "What are you pinching me for?"

"Play nice," she growled.

Regan removed a cream puff from the refrigerator and delicately placed it before Brandon. "I'm going to miss you, dude."

"Regan," Hyland announced firmly while glaring at him then motioned at those sitting at the table. "There are others who enjoy cream puffs."

Regan groaned, removed the platter from the refrigerator, and placed it on the table. Ellis immediately snatched a coveted cream puff.

"There goes tomorrow's dessert," Regan muttered.

Jacklyn turned to Brandon on her right and offered a pleasant smile. "So you've been working here for two years, huh?"

Hyland casually leaned back in his chair and eyed Brandon behind Jacklyn.

Brandon noted the look he received from his boss then offered a tense smile at Jacklyn. "It's going to look like an accident; you know that?"

Brandon's eyes strayed to meet Hyland's gaze and twisted smile. Jacklyn reached behind her. Hyland again yelped.

"Never mind the major," she announced firmly. "He doesn't tell me whom I can talk to." She cast a glare at her uncle. "We *discussed* it."

Hyland immediately tensed and stood. "Well, I think I'll be turning in," he announced a little too quickly then leaned down to kiss Jacklyn on the cheek. "Don't stay up too late, dear."

They watched Hyland kiss Jacklyn then head upstairs by the back stairs.

Brandon appeared confused and looked around. "Did I miss something?"

"Never teach a child your dirtiest combat moves if you don't intend for her to use them," Ellis casually remarked.

"No way," Regan cried out while looking at Jacklyn. "You did *that* to the major?"

Jacklyn smiled and shrugged.

"I get the 'stay away from my niece' lecture every time you visit," Brandon announced.

"I got that lecture once," Regan informed him then looked at Jacklyn. "I told him unless you turned into a cream pie, he had nothing to worry about."

"He even threatened me once," Ellis muttered from the sink.

Everyone stared at Ellis with surprise by the comment and watched him rinse dishes.

"Dude," Regan cried out. "What did you say?"

"I told him if he ever suggested something like that again," Ellis announced, "I'd heist his kidney while he slept, fry it up, and serve it to him in his scrambled eggs."

All three stared at Ellis with shock.

"Forget the major," Regan gasped. "Let's not piss off Ellis."

"My father was Uncle Hyland's best friend, and my mother was his little sister," she announced to the others. "I think he feels the need to protect me."

"I certainly hope you warned your boyfriend about him," Brandon remarked. "He'll eat him for breakfast."

"You mean Simon?" she asked with surprise then laughed. "We're just friends. He's a little too eccentric for me."

"He's beyond eccentric," Brandon informed her while shaking his head. "I found him at the crime scene acting like he'd seen a ghost."

"I've totally seen ghosts, man," Regan announced as his eyes widened.

"You're a little old to believe in ghosts," Ellis scolded.

Regan cast a glare at Ellis across the kitchen. "They don't appear to people like you."

"You mean sane people?" Ellis mocked.

Jacklyn sank into thought and was now distracted by what Brandon had told her. Brandon stared at her a moment then caressed her hand on her lap.

"I'm sorry," he announced. "I didn't mean to upset you. I'm sure he just had too much to drink."

Jacklyn eyed his hand that now caressed hers and met his gaze.

He smiled timidly and removed his hand. "And I should probably stop doing that."

Regan stared at him with surprise. "Dude, were you just feeling her leg?"

§

Loud piano music was heard pulsating throughout the north wing ballroom. A candelabra flickered on top of the grand piano while Simon played the energetic tune with strong, hard fingers striking the keys. Faint laughter was heard from deep within the room. Flickering ghostly silhouettes appeared to glide and twirl across the dusty ballroom floor.

Chapter Thirteen

Sunlight flooded Jacklyn's large bedroom suite through the part in the heavy curtains. Jacklyn woke, shielded her eyes from the sun, and then turned away from the sunlight, wanting to sleep another hour or more. She nestled on her side then felt a cool breeze followed by someone brushing a stray lock of hair from her brow. She opened her eyes but didn't see anyone by her bedside. Jacklyn then noticed Simon across the room sleeping slumped in the corner on the floor despite a vacant chair not five feet from him. She stared at him a moment with surprise and uncertainly sat up in her bed.

"Simon?"

Simon slowly woke and looked around while straightening with some stiffness. He appeared slightly disoriented.

"Hmm?" He ran his fingers through his hair and smiled with embarrassment. "Oh, I'm sorry. I didn't want to be alone. I must have dozed off."

"Are you okay?" she asked with concern, wondering how long he'd been asleep on the floor in her bedroom. "Brandon said you had an episode at the crime scene last night."

Simon's expression immediately dropped. "That bastard," he snarled then sprang up from the floor. "I'm fine. I should probably shower and change." He hurried from the room to avoid further conversation.

§

The massive sunroom contained an entire wall of floor to ceiling windows, allowing sunlight to flood the entire room. The old hardwood floor had seen better days and possibly had been carpeted prior to the architect taking up residence. Brandon sat before the drafting table and sketched within the sunlight. Jacklyn entered the room and looked around, marveling at the room beyond what was now the architect's office. She focused her attention on Brandon, who just noticed her presence.

"I hope I'm not disturbing you," she announced while offering a tiny smile.

He set his colored pencils down and straightened while grinning. "I have two years to finish," he announced cheerfully. "I can spare a few minutes."

Jacklyn approached and glanced at the drawings and photos spread out on his drafting table. There were photos of different rooms with penciled sketches alongside them showing perceived modifications.

"I thought architects were all about blueprints," she announced while casting a glance at him.

Brandon picked up a roll of blueprints and waved it. "Have some of those too," he announced while grinning. "I'm less of an architect and more of an interior decorator with a destructive side." He resumed sketching. "I wanted to be an artist, but I wasn't eccentric or insane enough. My architect background kept me employed but miserable. When your uncle offered me this job, I jumped on it."

Jacklyn eyed the nearby sketchpad then indicated it while glancing at him. "May I?"

"Sure," he replied and grinned. "My offensive sketches are in my room."

She turned the sketchpad to reveal a drawing of Regan leaning on the counter half-asleep with a cup of coffee.

"It's Regan," she announced cheerfully. "Too cute."

"Think your friend would mind flying me over the island for some aerial shots?" Brandon asked while casting a glance at her. "I'd be willing to pay him."

"I'm sure he would, but he won't take your money," she informed him. "You can't be that eccentric without being rich." Jacklyn set the pad down and approached the wall of windows. "Ocean view. Impressive."

"So what brings you to the south wing?" Brandon asked. "Regan need another spider killed?"

Jacklyn sat on a table near the window while Brandon continued to sketch. "No, I did that already," she teased then turned serious. "Simon is acting strange, well, stranger than usual. He has this distant look in his eyes like there's no one home." She studied Brandon. "He's been that way ever since we found the dead woman."

"Dealing with insanity is more Regan's department," Brandon replied. "He lives closer to it than I do."

Brandon continued to sketch with moderate enthusiasm. Jacklyn appeared curious then stood and began to approach him. He held his hand up to stop her. She found it odd that she actually obeyed his silent command. He finished sketching then turned the pad to her. It was a drawing of her against the table in a short skirt and low cut shirt.

She eyed the sketch then snorted a soft laugh. "Nice, but my boobs aren't that big."

"I didn't want to stare," he teased.

Regan entered with a thermos of coffee and a paper bag. He approached the drafting table and handed them to Brandon. "Dude, you forgot your take-out."

"I hoped if I waited long enough, you'd deliver," Brandon teased.

Regan eyed the sketch and shook his head with disapproval. "Boobs are too big, man," he announced, "but at least you drew clothing this time."

Brandon shut the pad and impatiently glared at him. "Something I can do for you?"

"Oh, I'm sorry. Did I interrupt something that Hyland might beat you for?" Regan announced in a slightly offended tone. He cast a look at Jacklyn and immediately grinned. "One time Hyland found, like, these naked drawings--"

"Regan, what do you want?" Brandon demanded, cutting his story short.

He glared at Brandon then looked at Jacklyn. "Simon's kind of freaking out," Regan informed her. "I thought maybe you'd like to know."

Chapter Fourteen

The cemetery, which was located beyond the lavish garden, contained nearly fifty old headstones and a modern crypt surrounded by tall weeping willow trees. Simon sat among the headstones with his knees to his chest and held his head while staring blankly at nothing. Ellis stood on the patio near the kitchen with his cup of coffee and seemed to keep close watch over Simon. Jacklyn, Brandon, and Regan approached Ellis.

"Is he still freaking out?" Regan asked.

"No, he's just sitting there talking to himself," Ellis remarked with little emotion.

"Thanks for keeping an eye on him," Jacklyn announced then debated her next move.

"I'm actually just waiting to see his head spin around again," Ellis informed her.

Jacklyn groaned with disapproval and left the patio. She approached Simon on the grass and crouched beside him while he stared at the crypt.

"Simon?" she announced gently while studying him. "Are you okay?"

"There's another one," he muttered without looking at her while rubbing his temples.

"Another what?"

"Another body," he replied. "In the crypt. He was stabbed in the abdomen."

"How do you know--?"

"He told me."

Jacklyn looked back at the others waiting on the patio. "Uh, a little help here."

All three hurried toward them, although it was unclear how they could help.

"If you have any sedatives, now would be a good time to break them out," Jacklyn announced to no one in particular but hoped someone had some.

Ellis nodded and helped Regan get Simon to his feet. Jacklyn stopped Brandon and indicated the crypt.

"We need to look in there," she announced timidly while staring at the crypt.

He gave her a surprised look. "What would you possibly want to see in there?"

Jacklyn stared with concern but didn't respond. Brandon groaned, approached the crypt, and then kicked in the door. The latch easily broke, and the door flew open with a thunderous crack. Dust and cobwebs gently floated to the ground.

"There should be a torch just inside," she informed him and shivered slightly.

"Sure, now you're afraid of the dark," Brandon muttered under his breath.

He reached inside for the torch and pulled out a decomposed arm. The rest of the dead man fell against him.   Brandon jumped back with a gasp and released the arm.

"Oh, shit!"

Jacklyn cried out and jumped back as well.   Both stared at the badly decomposed body.   Large spiders scattered from the body's tattered old-time gangster costume and crawled across Brandon.   He batted them off.

"Son-of-a-bitch!"

"Simon said the dead guy told him he was in there," she gasped while staring at the decayed body.

Brandon swatted another spider off him and glared at Jacklyn.   "Did he also mention the corpse would fall on whoever opened the door?"

"No," she replied timidly.   "He failed to supply that information."

Chapter Fifteen

Nearly an hour later, the police milled around the crypt containing the body just outside the open door. Detective Reed stood with Jacklyn, Ellis, Regan, and Brandon on the garden path just within view of the family crypt.

"He was killed around the same time as the woman in the bathtub," Detective Reed informed them.

"Nine years ago," Ellis remarked.

Detective Reed stared at Ellis with some surprise. "How did you know?"

"There were only two costume parties," he announced. "One was nineteen years ago and the other nine. So it had to be the last one."

"Yes, of course, you're correct."

"Of course I am," Ellis replied. "That particular party was on Columbus Day. There were one hundred and twenty guests in attendance, twenty wait staff, and two bartenders. Over twenty pounds of caviar was served." He sharply eyed Regan. "Four of which never made it to the ballroom."

Regan avoided looking at Ellis.

He then returned his attention to Detective Reed and raised a clever brow. "Would you like to know how many cases of champagne were opened?"

"No, that won't be necessary." The detective held up a sealed bag containing a woman's gypsy costume and feathery Mardi Gras mask. "At least we know what happened to the dead woman's clothes. We found these on the crypt floor. She was with our male victim in the crypt, probably doing something kinky, when the killer stabbed her lover. He probably chased her into that room." His look turned stern. "I'll need to talk to the guy who had the premonition."

"He's been heavily sedated," Ellis responded. "I'll get you a copy of that guest list."

Ellis and the detective headed to the mansion with Regan following.

Brandon caught Jacklyn's hand, stopped her, and gave her a serious look. "You're lucky I didn't tell the detective about Simon's behavior last night."

"And I appreciate that," Jacklyn remarked.

Hyland was heard clearing his throat from nearby. Brandon pulled his hand from Jacklyn's hand.

Hyland smirked with an almost accusing look. "Taking the day off, Brandon?"

"Just taking a fifteen-minute 'decayed body' break," he replied casually.

"Why were you even out here?" Hyland practically demanded while glaring at Brandon.

"He was helping me with Simon."

"If you need assistance with something, see Ellis or Regan," Hyland sternly informed his niece. "Brandon has his own work."

Jacklyn folded her arms across her chest and glared at her uncle with hostility. "I can associate with whomever I choose."

"I'm not telling you with whom you can associate," Hyland corrected with some anger. "I'm telling Brandon to do his job, not my niece."

"That was uncalled for," Brandon snarled.

"I'd say it's completely called for," he snapped then held up the sketch of Jacklyn. "I told you about your pornographic drawings, and then I find this."

"That's completely innocent," Brandon informed him. "You're overreacting."

"Overreacting?"

"That's enough," Jacklyn cried out in anger. "You need to stop this overly protective behavior, Uncle Hyland, or I'm leaving here and never coming back."

Hyland was about to speak.

"And if that happens, you'd better believe I'll sleep with him before I go," she launched hotly.

Hyland appeared shocked while staring back at her. Jacklyn's glare was stern as her eyes locked onto her uncle's eyes.

Brandon took another step back and appeared horrified. "I am so dead."

"Fine, I'll back off," Hyland announced, "but ask him to show you his private stash."

As Hyland returned to the mansion, Jacklyn stared after him with some confusion then turned and glared at Brandon.

He held his hands in the air and backed up another step. "Just let me explain--"

"Explain what?" she snapped hotly while staring at him with a horrified expression on her face. "What did you do?"

Brandon considered the question then fidgeted. "Give me a minute." He met her gaze with some concern. "I may have sketched you nude."

Her eyes widened in horror as she gasped, "Where did you get the pictures?"

"No pictures--just my imagination."

There was an awkward silence. Jacklyn immediately relaxed and managed a soft laugh. "Oh, is that all?" she announced then waved him off. "I assure you my uncle's done worse in his lifetime."

Brandon stared at her with surprise and raised his brows. "So you're okay with it?"

Jacklyn took his arm and guided him to the kitchen patio. "Seventy percent of my friends are guys," she casually informed him. "Almost all have made at least one obscene proposition, told me about some vulgar dream, or copped a feel. Nude sketches are mild."

"Which category did Simon fall under?"

She reluctantly sighed. "Sadly, all three."

"Simon copped a feel?"

"In his defense, he was very drunk at the time," she announced.

"Just for the record," he asked while glancing at her. "What's the penalty for an unsolicited kiss?"

"Too many variables," she insisted. "Some obnoxious guy in a bar would suffer severely, while a friend might only receive a harsh stare."

Brandon turned to face her with a tiny smile. "There's one variable you've overlooked."

"Oh? And what's that?" she asked with a curious look.

"Diversion."

Brandon kissed her quickly on the lips then took off. She watched him head for the south wing. He glanced back and smiled slyly. Jacklyn laughed and headed for the mansion, entering the kitchen from the patio. Ellis and Regan stood by the window glaring at her with their arms folded across their chests as Jacklyn walked past them.

"I don't want to hear it," she announced firmly without looking at either.

Ellis followed her and Regan followed him. "I seem to recall a certain duke attempting to kiss you, and, if I remember correctly, you slapped him," Ellis announced with irritation. "A duke, Jacklyn, you slapped a duke, but you let the hired help kiss you."

"He kissed me and ran. Should I have chased him?" she demanded. "That'd be real classy."

"As classy as say slapping a duke?" Ellis scoffed.

Jacklyn groaned and continued across the kitchen. Ellis remained on her heels.

"That was five years ago," Jacklyn remarked. "I can't believe you're still harping on that."

"What part of 'duke' aren't you understanding?" Ellis demanded.

Jacklyn took a bottle of water from the refrigerator. When she turned, Ellis and Regan glared at her with their arms across their chests.

Jacklyn glared at Regan and the look on his face. "Are you pissed about the duke too?"

"Four years ago, I asked to kiss you," he announced, "and you totally turned me down."

"I'm trapped in a nightmare," she muttered.

Jacklyn approached Regan, grabbed him by the face, and kissed him on the lips. She pulled back and glared at him.

"Are you happy?"

Regan stared at her with surprise and could barely speak. "Uh, yeah, I'm good."

Jacklyn turned to Ellis, grabbed him by the face, and kissed him quickly but passionately on the mouth. Ellis immediately tensed by the kiss. Jacklyn pulled away and glared at him.

"Give that to the duke with my sincere apologies," she announced.

Jacklyn left the kitchen. Regan and Ellis stared after her in silence. Neither man moved.

"What an awesome day," Regan announced then grinned.

"I need a cold shower," Ellis declared with little expression then left the kitchen.

Chapter Sixteen

Hyland sat behind his desk in the study with an actual dart gun in his hand. He shot darts from the gun across the room into a dartboard located near the door. Each dart made a distinct hiss as it was expelled from the gun. There was a soft knock on the study door.

"Come in."

Jacklyn entered the study. The gun hissed as another dart struck the dartboard. Jacklyn shut the door and observed the small darts in the center of the board alongside the door.

"That's a new spin on an old game," she remarked with some disapproval.

"Ellis got cranky when I used the twenty-two," he muttered.

Jacklyn approached his desk and paused less than a foot away from him. "Can we talk or should I fear being shot with a poison dart?"

"Don't be silly," he announced firmly. "They're tranquilizers."

Jacklyn sat on the edge of the desk near him. "I'm sorry if I upset you this morning."

"Sorry you upset me, but not about what you said," he remarked while casting a glance at her.

"I could have been less surly."

Hyland glared at her. "That wasn't surly that was snarly."

"I learned from the best."

"Yeah, your mother was a bit snarly too," he commented.

Jacklyn glared at him. He caught her stare, hid his smile, and shot another dart into the dartboard. He set the dart gun down on the desk and turned in his chair to face her.

"You wouldn't really sleep with Brandon just to spite me, would you?" he asked.

"I wouldn't even leave forever just to spite you," she announced with a tiny smile. "He confessed about the drawings he'd done. They were all imagination. You did overreact."

"Maybe, but he still thinks of you that way," Hyland remarked.

Jacklyn moved onto the arm of his chair and clung to him. "He's allowed to be attracted to me."

He glared at her. "Says who?"

"Says me," she replied. "One day someone will have to be if I'm ever going to marry."

He reluctantly groaned. "I would like to marry you off one day, so I suppose I should be a little more tolerant." He hesitated and met her gaze. "Would it make you happy if I apologized to Brandon?"

"That would be very mature of you."

He made a face. "Yeah, I hate having to act mature," her uncle muttered then sighed. "But if it makes you happy--"

There was a brief knock on the door before Ellis poked his head inside. "They're here."

Hyland groaned and rolled his eyes. "Wonderful," he snarled. "Lock up the booze."

"Already done," Ellis replied.

Chapter Seventeen

Harry Brighton entered the foyer with his daughter, Tara. Tara was the same age as Jacklyn. Their age was the only thing the two had in common. Tara was a short, petite woman with long, golden-brown hair. She wore a low-cut, lightweight tank top without a bra, which allowed for a generous view of her perky breasts through the thin fabric. Her cut-off jean shorts barely covered her ass and her hot pink, thong panties could be seen above the low waistband of the shorts. She capped off her outfit with strapless high heels.

Tara's father, Harry, was a reserved man, so the family often wondered what he thought of his daughter's trailer park trash wardrobe. Harry had short, light brown hair, and a clean-shaven face. He was moderately attractive for a man in his mid-fifties, although years of drinking seemed to have aged him beyond his actual years. Despite his heavy cologne, the strong smell of booze seemed to ooze from his pours. Dark circles beneath his eyes indicated he probably hadn't slept much last night and was possibly hungover from a drinking binge.

Harry's son, Derek, entered the foyer while clinging to a voluptuous, raven-haired beauty. Danika was the type of sexy Tara was striving to achieve but fell flat. Danika had a curvy body with a generous bosom and backside. Although she could have stepped out of the pages of a girly magazine, she dressed moderately conservative, leaving more to the imagination. She only wore a thin layer of makeup to achieve her timeless beauty. Her long hair was pinned back to contain the wild locks. Although her skirt was sleek against her curves, the hem reached just above her knees, and her blouse, although slightly see-through, only allowed a peek at her lacy bra beneath.

Derek was obviously proud of his newly acquired girlfriend and couldn't take his hands off her. With his average looks and a body that had never exercised, Danika was way out of his league. Derek looked like a younger, more attractive version of his father, but it was obvious he did little to better himself both physically and outwardly. He wore expensive clothes but didn't take time to keep them pressed as Simon had his clothes. He looked almost as if he'd fallen out of bed that morning and into his clothing.

Ellis appeared in the foyer a moment later, heaving four bags inside. Leanne stumbled in behind him with another four. Hyland and Jacklyn walked along the grand hallway from the study and approached the foyer. Hyland stopped and stared at his guests and their luggage.

"My God, they're moving in," Hyland scoffed.

Jacklyn nudged her uncle. "You promised," she scolded.

Tara saw Jacklyn, ran to her, and enthusiastically hugged her. Jacklyn returned the embrace, having not seen her cousin in some time.

"Ellis didn't say you'd be here," Tara squawked with giddy delight.

"It was a last minute decision," Jacklyn announced cheerfully and indicated her bags. "Why don't I help you get settled then we can talk over tea."

"Tea? Hell, girl, I want something stronger," Tara exclaimed with enthusiasm.

"I second that," Harry announced.

Both Tara and Derek gave their Uncle Hyland warm embraces, which he promptly returned. Derek then proudly displayed his sexy girlfriend.

"Uncle Hyland, this is my girlfriend, Danika," he announced while happily introducing the attractive, young woman.

"It's a pleasure, my dear," Hyland announced politely and attempted not to stare, although she easily caught his eye.

"Derek wasn't exaggerating, was he?" Danika remarked while looking around and marveling at the mansion. "This place really is like a castle."

"And twice as drafty," Hyland informed her.

Harry extended his hand to Hyland, who uncertainly accepted it. Harry pulled him in for a hug. Hyland made a face and politely pulled away.

"Good to see you, old man," Harry announced cheerfully while slapping his shoulder.

"You're older than me," Hyland muttered while holding back his sneer.

Jacklyn took two bags from Leanne, who appeared grateful and followed Jacklyn and Tara up the stairs. Ellis struggled with the remaining four bags. Hyland glared at Derek and Harry.

"Hey, guys. Ellis isn't the bellhop," Hyland remarked then snapped his fingers. Ellis dropped the bags on cue. "Carry your own damned bags."

Chapter Eighteen

Tara's bedroom chamber was similar to Jacklyn's but with a flowery sort of theme. Apart from looking like a gaudy garden exploded inside the room, the furniture and layout were almost identical to Jacklyn's room. Tara flopped onto the massive bed and looked at her cousin as she opened the curtains.

"So let's have it," Tara announced cheerfully. "Any prospects? Are you beating the hot guys off with a stick? Give me all the lusty details."

"Sorry, there are no lusty details," Jacklyn replied with humor. "What about you?"

"I'm happily single at the moment," she announced cheerfully. "I'm actually hoping to have a couple of wild nights with that amazingly cute architect." She offered a lustful grin and raised her brows seductively.

Jacklyn suddenly tensed and stared at her cousin. "Oh?" she asked with surprise. "You two have a thing going on?"

"There's some sexual tension," Tara informed her then giggled, "but it's still only in the flirting stages. I intend to change that this weekend."

"I see," Jacklyn replied while shifting with unfounded nervousness. "Uh, why don't you get settled, and I'll meet you in the game room for drinks."

§

Simon slouched in an oversized chair within the lounge with his hand to his temple and a glazed over look in his eyes. The massive sitting room had a definite woman's touch, having been decorated by the late Lady Brighton. It had been one of her favorite rooms. In addition to the antique, Victorian furniture, there were many expensive vases, and artwork handpicked by the lady of the house as well. The room, like many of the rooms, contained a stone fireplace and framed photos lined the marble mantel.

Lady Brighton's portrait hung above the fireplace as if overseeing her cherished room. Jacklyn's Aunt Mara had been a stunning woman with long, blonde hair and a flawless, silky white complexion. Sunlight flooded the room through the large windows along the entire wall. Jacklyn sat on the coffee table before Simon, glad he was coming out of his drug-induced coma.

"Simon?"

"Hmm?" he responded without looking at her and just stared at the coffee table.

"Want to tell me what happened this morning?" she gently asked.

"You're going to think I'm crazy."

"Too late," she chirped. "Now you need to convince me that you're not."

"Why do I feel so numb?" Simon asked while attempting to feel his hands.

"Ellis gave you a special cocktail to sedate you," she informed him.

Brandon entered the lounge, appeared annoyed, and sat on the arm of the sofa. "I thought you were going to tell me when he was awake?"

She ignored him. "I'm worried, Simon," Jacklyn gently remarked. "Talk to me."

He hesitated, drew a deep breath, and contemplated his next words. "When I was little, I realized I could talk to the dead. Unsettled spirits," he finally blurted out. "I've learned to live in my own hell and even accepted it, but when it comes to violent deaths, I see things I wish I didn't."

"Oh, God, he's insane," Brandon muttered while rolling his eyes in response.

Jacklyn swatted Brandon's leg near her and looked back at Simon. "I believe you."

"You do?" he suddenly asked with surprise. Simon took her hands and appeared serious while staring into her eyes. "I'm so glad to hear you say that. Your parents insisted I come here with you."

"Insane," Brandon remarked while shaking his head. "I told you so."

"That's not funny, Simon," Jacklyn announced then walked away from him and looked at a picture of her parents on the fireplace mantel.

Simon jumped up from his chair and approached her. "How do you think we met?" he insisted. "They sought me out and sent me to you."

She spun to face him with hostility and anger on her face. "Stop it."

"I can't stop it! I'm not doing it," he shouted back. "They feared for your life, Jacklyn. Whoever killed them is coming after you!"

"They died in a car accident! I told you that," she launched with anger then shook her head while fighting her emotions. "Why are you doing this?"

"I can prove it."

Brandon suddenly stepped between them and pushed Simon away. "That's enough," he snarled. "You're upsetting her!"

Simon drifted out a second then looked at Jacklyn. "Your mother says she liked the flowered dress you buried her in, but she wishes you'd kept your grandmother's pearls," he announced then appeared confused. "They were fake?"

Jacklyn stared at him with surprise and near horror. "She never told anyone that," she gasped then moved closer to him. "You really are talking to her!"

"He's conning you, Jacklyn," Brandon insisted while shaking his head.

Simon spun around and glared at Brandon. "Don't piss off the dead," he snarled and pointed a demanding finger at him. "Contrary to popular belief, they can hurt the living."

"Don't trust him, Jacklyn," Brandon warned her then left the room.

Jacklyn moved closer to Simon. "What did they say about the accident?"

"Your father saw someone standing in the road just before something struck the windshield," he informed her. "The image won't let him rest."

"What makes him think I'm in danger?"

Simon hesitated then subconsciously rubbed his temples and shook his head. "He's not making any sense," he announced while attempting to understand what he was hearing. "He says your uncle knows something but doesn't realize it." He then looked at her with concern. "When he figures it out, you're both in danger."

Chapter Nineteen

Jacklyn approached Regan while he enthusiastically prepared dinner for that evening. Ellis placed table settings consisting of the fine china and silverware onto the rolling waiter. It was obvious he wasn't nearly as enthusiastic as the jolly cook.

"You seem more cheerful than usual this evening," Jacklyn announced while watching Regan cook. "What's the occasion?"

"I'm cooking a gourmet dinner for ten. I love formal dinner parties," he announced with enthusiasm. "I hardly ever get to prepare gourmet dishes anymore. I spent all afternoon on chocolate mousse with raspberries. It's exciting."

Ellis rolled his eyes and resumed placing dishes on the rolling cart. "Yes, it's very exciting," he muttered. "More time for Uncle Harry to berate the staff."

"Don't let him push your buttons, Ellis," she casually announced while folding her arms across her chest. "You know he's an asshole."

She received stray looks and grins from both men at the blunt comment. She then seemed to consider something and gave a curious look.

"Who are the other three?" Jacklyn asked while silently counting guests in her head.

"Your uncle invited Brandon and Rick," Ellis informed her.

"I guess Tara asked that Brandon be invited," Jacklyn remarked while frowning.

"Oh, goody, dinner and a show," Ellis muttered under his breath.

Jacklyn stared at him with a puzzled look. Regan noted her look and felt compelled to respond.

"When your cousin drinks, no man is safe," Regan chimed in.

Hyland entered the kitchen and seemed unusually cheerful considering his unplanned weekend guests. "Jacklyn, would you get three bottles of Merlot from the wine cellar?" he announced then immediately made a face. "Not the good stuff. Harry will just guzzle it down like grape juice. I have to set place cards."

"I can do that," Ellis offered.

"No, I want to," Hyland insisted. "Hurry with those dishes."

"Dude, dinner won't be ready for another hour," Regan informed him. "You can't rush duck."

Hyland ignored him and hurried from the room. All three watched him depart and offered matching strange looks.

"Who wants to check Uncle Harry's seat for booby traps?" Jacklyn teased.

"He's on his own," Ellis remarked.

§

The dining room was elegant yet moderately tacky with big, bold carpeting and brilliant, hunter green painted walls. The thick, massive dining room table could comfortably seat twelve guests on broad, pedestal leg chairs. The table was set for ten guests with the good china, crystal glasses, and the expensive silverware. There was a large flower arrangement in the center of the table and several candles in brass candlesticks placed along the middle. That evening, everyone followed Hyland into the dining room. Regan, Ellis, and Leanne stood prepared to serve covered dishes on awaiting, wooden carts. Rick and Brandon were the last to enter. They softly bantered while fidgeting with their ties. Neither man was used to formal dinner parties, and it showed.

"If everyone will find their assigned seat, we can get started," Hyland announced cheerfully.

Hyland took his place at the head of the table. Harry looked at the second head of the table for his name and appeared surprised he wasn't seated there. Hyland looked at his two nieces and patted the chair to his left.

"Jacklyn, dear, you're to my left," Hyland announced then looked at Tara and grinned. "And, Tara, you're to my right."

Harry was seated at the far end, putting as much distance from Hyland as possible. Derek was to his father's right with Danika seated alongside him. Brandon was seated next to Jacklyn and Simon next to Tara. Rick was seated between Harry and Simon. The second head of the table remained vacant.

"So who's this special guest?" Jacklyn asked.

"Ellis," Hyland announced and indicated the seat at the opposite end of the table. "Please join us."

Everyone including Ellis appeared surprised by the invitation. He uncertainly took the seat at the opposite end. Regan and Leanne hid their grins and served the platters to the guests.

As Regan served Ellis his covered dinner plate, he grinned slyly. "Sir--"

Ellis covered his mouth with his fingers and muttered to Regan, "Ladies first."

Regan appeared embarrassed. "Oops."

Chapter Twenty

Everyone had a good time during dinner, although Tara snubbed Simon throughout most of the meal. Rick and Brandon engaged Ellis in conversation, helping him not feel quite so out of place.

Hyland leaned closer to Jacklyn and grinned. "I thought inviting Brandon to dinner would make you happy," he announced just loud enough for her to hear. "Pretty mature on my behalf, if I do say so."

"Yes, I'm proud of you."

"So, Uncle Hyland," Derek announced. "What sort of exciting things have you done to the place?"

"Brandon has some wonderful ideas for the south wing," Hyland replied. "Maybe if you beg, he'll let you have a peek."

Tara eyed Brandon and smiled lustfully. "I'm not above begging."

Brandon didn't even acknowledge Tara's comment and focused his attention on Derek. "I can show you some finished sketches for the conservatory."

While they discussed the plans for the conservatory, Brandon placed his hand on Jacklyn's hand resting on her lap, surprising her.

"What about the north wing?" Harry asked. "That could use some major work."

Brandon chuckled in his throat. "I can't even mention the north wing--"

"Shh," Hyland scolded.

"See," Brandon remarked.

"We have another two years on the south wing," Hyland announced in a weary tone. "I'm not even thinking about the north wing right now."

"You'd be amazed at what we could--" Brandon began.

"Shh," Hyland immediately silenced him.

"Give it up, Brandon," Rick announced. "We'll discuss it again in two years."

"Renovating that wing would be sacrilegious," Simon suddenly chimed in.

All eyes were on Simon.

"A good cleaning, a little wax, some stain, and it'll be breathtaking," Simon remarked. "You don't need plumbing and electric. Renovating it will ruin it."

Hyland stared at Simon a moment then grinned. "I like his idea," he announced. "It doesn't cost nearly as much as Brandon's."

"There's a big difference between the north and south wing," Brandon announced. "Some hippy contractor from the sixties made the south wing the abomination it is today."

"Oh, so we actually agree on something?" Simon remarked.

Jacklyn eyed Brandon's fingers caressing hers.

Hyland leaned back in his chair and studied Simon. "Perhaps you and Brandon could walk the north wing, compare notes, and show me something on paper."

Simon stared at him with surprise. "You want me to advise you on restoring the north wing?"

"Think of it more as a consultation."

"I'd love that," Simon announced while smiling with enthusiasm.

Brandon's hand slipped under Jacklyn's hand and caressed it with his thumb while he grinned at her. "Are you up for a creepy adventure in the north wing with us?" he asked.

"Someone should supervise you two," she teased.

"My God, we're back in fifth grade playing hide-and-seek in the dungeon looking for pirates' treasure," Tara scoffed. "I would think grown men could find better things to occupy their time."

"You're just jealous because you weren't invited to play with us," Simon snapped.

"Why would I want to hang out in that disgusting, dirty rattrap?" Tara asked.

"You'll discover one day not to judge a book by its cover," Simon casually informed her.

"Are we still talking about dirty old buildings?" Tara demanded.

Ellis studied the wine in his glass. Hyland seemed to be the only one aware of his strange behavior.

"Are you still with us, Ellis?" Hyland asked.

"Merlot 1998. Half the vineyard was destroyed by a drought that year," Ellis informed his boss. "This is the cheapest wine in the cellar, yet it's being served in a three-hundred dollar, crystal glass."

"Is he okay?" Danika asked with concern.

Ellis looked at Danika past the glass. "Just making Simon's point. You can serve cheap wine in an expensive glass, but it's still just cheap wine."

Simon held his glass up to Ellis in agreement. Jacklyn eyed Brandon's hand caressing hers then looked away and returned the caress.

"Excellent meal, Regan," Hyland announced then looked at his guests. "Who's up for drinks and a friendly game of pool?"

"I wouldn't mind a couple of drinks," Harry eagerly replied.

"I'm game," Rick chimed in.

Everyone stood. Brandon released Jacklyn's hand and pulled her chair out for her. Ellis attempted to help collect dishes when Hyland slapped him on the back and smirked.

"Leave that," Hyland announced. "You're a guest tonight."

Ellis appeared out of place but left the dirty dishes. He looked at Regan, who smiled and gave him a thumbs up.

Chapter Twenty-one

While the others headed into the game room for drinks, Jacklyn led Brandon into the study across the hall from the dining room and shut the door. As she turned to face him, he moved closer to her and nearly trapped her against the door.

"Am I in trouble?" he teased.

Jacklyn shifted uncomfortably and placed her hand on his chest to maintain distance between them. Her look was stern and serious.

"I know about you and Tara, and I'm not comfortable with this game," she announced, leaving little room for explanation.

He stared at her with some surprise. "Me and Tara?" he suddenly asked. "I'm confused. I only met her once, and we barely spoke."

"She implied that the two of you were in the flirting stages of a relationship," Jacklyn informed him and raised her brows. "She said she came alone thinking you would have a weekend fling."

He stared at her a moment as if confused then immediately shook his head. "No, she came alone because she's intolerable," Brandon pointed out with little hesitation. "Even your friend Simon can't stand her, and he likes everyone. During her last visit, she was so wasted; she came on to every man in the room." He stared into her eyes. "She was like a mutt in heat. She was so bad, Regan hid in the kitchen all night."

Jacklyn knew her cousin was a bit flirty and had spent plenty of time in the company of countless men, but she would never have suspected she was as aggressive as everyone was suddenly claiming. She didn't want to think bad thoughts about her cousin.

Brandon moved closer to Jacklyn and smiled warmly. "There's nothing between Tara and me," he insisted, "and I've never been the slightest bit interested in her. I was too busy lusting after you."

He lowered his mouth to hers and gently kissed her. Jacklyn felt her heart pounding as she eagerly returned the kiss. Brandon kissed her more passionately as they fell against the door with a thump. The door vibrated from the other end.

"Hey," Regan called from the other side of the door. "Is someone in there?"

Jacklyn broke off the kiss and hid her embarrassed smile. "We should probably join the others."

"Yeah, the last thing I need is Hyland standing over me with a shotgun," Brandon remarked.

When she opened the door, Regan stood in the doorway with his arms folded across his chest and his eyebrows raised.

"You two need a chaperone--seriously," he announced firmly.

As Regan walked away, Jacklyn was about to head for the game room. Brandon caught her hand and stopped her. She met his gaze and noted his boyish grin.

"How about a moonlit walk on the beach first?" he suggested. "I'm not too anxious to join the others."

"Actually, I'd like that very much," Jacklyn replied.

Brandon held her hand and led her down the hallway toward the foyer.

Chapter Twenty-two

Within the game room, Harry bartended for Tara, Derek, and Danika. The bar was a dark mahogany with enough seating for fifteen guests and the back shelf held several dozen bottles of top-shelf alcohol. The slate top pool table had thick, pedestal legs and a red liner rather than the traditional green. Hyland and Rick played a friendly game of pool, although neither appeared particularly friendly. Ellis and Simon sat at one of several pub tables and watched the game from a safe distance.

In addition to the pool table, there was also a felt top poker table, several vintage slot machines, and a pinball machine that was clearly out-of-place in the room. Several sofas and chairs were set up around a large, flat screen television mounted on the back wall. Jacklyn and Brandon entered the room more than an hour later and eyed the others from the doorway. Jacklyn turned to face Brandon and gave him a serious look.

"Before I talk to Tara, you understand you're passing up a sure thing for a 'what might be in the future' thing," she bravely informed him.

"Get her plastered and gift wrap her for Ellis," Brandon announced with little concern. "He's the one who needs a sure thing. I just want a chance with you."

Brandon warmly kissed her hand then headed for the pool table. Jacklyn drew a deep breath and approached Tara at the bar.

"What can I get for you, honey?" Harry asked.

"Vodka and cranberry juice," she replied then sat alongside Tara, who watched the game with interest. "So, who's winning?"

"Well, considering one player works for the other, less forgiving player, I'd say Uncle Hyland is winning," Tara teased. "I'm actually only interested in the hot stud who just walked in."

Jacklyn appeared uncomfortable and sipped the strong drink. "Tara, I don't really know how to say this," she announced timidly, "but Brandon and I are sort of seeing each other."

Tara shot a look at her and appeared stunned. "What? But you said--"

"I didn't mention it earlier because I thought maybe I'd misread his interest," Jacklyn explained, "but it turns out that's not the case."

"Well, he certainly sent some pretty strong signals last time I visited," Tara snapped hotly.

"Perhaps he did," Jacklyn easily lied, "but things have changed since then."

"We'll just see about that," Tara cried out. "He'll reconsider when he hears you don't put out!"

Tara jumped from her bar stool and headed for the pool table. Jacklyn groaned and followed. As they approached, a drunken Ellis shied away from Tara and stood behind Simon.

Tara placed her hand on Brandon's shoulder and smiled lustfully. "Could we talk somewhere private?"

"I'm good right here," Brandon replied with little interest.

Ellis muttered to Simon over his shoulder, "We may have to sacrifice Brandon to save ourselves."

Tara folded her arms across her chest while glaring at Brandon. "You can't honestly tell me you'd rather be with Jacklyn, who doesn't put out, than with me."

"I'm not interested in you, Tara," Brandon informed her. "I *am* interested in Jacklyn. Not being easy makes her more attractive."

Hyland appeared curious and approached Brandon from behind.

Brandon tensed and eyed Jacklyn. "Hyland is behind me, isn't he?"

Jacklyn smiled and nodded.

Tara remained hostile and annoyed. "Well, I hate to tell you, but she doesn't inherit the mansion or the island," she scoffed as her eyes narrowed. "It reverts back to my father. So you're wasting your time."

"What makes you think I care about any of that?" Brandon demanded. "You'd be shocked at what Hyland pays me."

Harry quickly approached the arguing couple. "Tara, you're embarrassing yourself."

She turned and glared at her father. "I'm embarrassing myself?" she launched in anger. "You're the one who drinks yourself into oblivion then comes on to the hired help."

"Unlike someone else who had to be pried off the butler," Ellis muttered just loud enough for Tara to hear.

Harry and Tara glared at Ellis.

He cleverly raised his brows. "That's how I remember it," Ellis commented.

Tara stormed from the room.

Ellis casually sipped his drink. "Was it something I said?"

"I'm sorry about her behavior," Harry announced. "She's had too much to drink. I'll talk to her."

Harry hurried after her. Hyland placed his hand on Brandon's shoulder. Brandon jerked and stiffened.

"I'm starting to enjoy this evening," Hyland announced cheerfully. "Let's get drunk."

"Way ahead of you, Major," Ellis cheerfully replied while raising his glass.

Hyland and Ellis returned to Rick at the pool table. Brandon moved closer to Jacklyn and watched the three men across the room.

"No sheep will be safe tonight," Brandon boldly announced. "Anyone want to ditch this frat party and take a dip in the hot tub?"

Chapter Twenty-three

The patio lights lit the pool and hot tub area between the house and the garden. The large, ten-person hot tub was built inground alongside the swimming pool. Both contained underwater lights to keep the area lit when patio lights weren't required. Brandon, Simon, Jacklyn, Regan, and Leanne lounged in the hot tub while sipping champagne. Jacklyn and Leanne wore conservative two-piece bathing suits. Simon and Brandon wore their swim trunks and went shirtless. Regan seemed self-conscious about his larger frame and wore a white t-shirt in the hot tub. They laughed and joked at Ellis' expense.

"Last time Ellis was drunk, he made me tango with him in the kitchen," Leanne informed them. "I couldn't keep his hand off my ass."

"Ellis is wound too tight," Regan replied. "When he gets drunk, he just kind of explodes."

"I'm more concerned about the major being so nice to me," Brandon muttered and shifted uncomfortably. "He's up to something."

"Stay out of Jacklyn's bed, dude," Regan informed him, "and you won't have to worry about it."

Simon suddenly laughed forcing Jacklyn to glare at him with a look of disapproval as if she knew what he was about to say.

"I can't imagine Jacklyn letting any man into her bed," Simon teased.

Leanne grinned and held back her laugh. "Is Jacklyn a good, little girl?"

"More or less," Jacklyn replied while grinning.

"I don't think there's much of a gray area here," Brandon teased while chuckling.

"Mostly good--with the occasional happy ending," Jacklyn responded.

Brandon, Regan, and Leanne suddenly laughed. Brandon pulled her to his side and kissed her. Simon became tense and stared into the distance, catching everyone's attention.

"Simon?" Jacklyn announced attempting to break his concerning trance.

Regan swatted his shoulder. Simon snapped out of his trance and yelped with surprise.

"You're freaking out the straights," Regan informed him with a stern look.

"What's going on?" Leanne suddenly asked.

"Dude sees, like, ghosts and stuff," Regan remarked then eyed Simon. "It's okay. I totally believe you. I see them too. I see specs of dancing light when I'm alone in the kitchen."

"Are you sure you're not suffering a stroke?" Brandon casually remarked.

"Seriously, dude? A fat joke?" Regan demanded. "With all those pastries you pack away--?"

Leanne turned her attention to Simon. "So tell us. What did you see?"

"It was Lady Brighton," Simon gently replied.

Everyone stared at Simon with shared looks of horror.

"Dude, don't ever say that in front of Hyland," Regan announced with concern.

"I hope you're not going to tell us she was murdered too," Brandon remarked.

"I couldn't say for sure," Simon remarked then hesitated, "but she seems to think she was."

Brandon gave Jacklyn a stern look.

"Lady Brighton died from a lingering heart condition," Leanne informed them. "They did an autopsy and everything."

"I think we'd better keep this ghost stuff between us," Jacklyn announced, directing her comment at Simon.

"I'm not making it up. She thinks she was slowly poisoned," Simon informed them. "If she died of natural causes, she wouldn't be here. What wealthy, fifty-year-old woman dies of natural causes?"

"She was kind of young," Regan remarked.

"She was in good shape too," Leanne muttered.

"And if she was poisoned slowly, that makes her killer Hyland, Ellis, or one of you two," Brandon bluntly announced while cleverly raising his brows.

"Jacklyn, dear, your boyfriend is getting a little cranky," Leanne announced and smiled daringly at her. "I think he needs a happy ending."

Regan chuckled. Jacklyn hid her smile.

"I can't be silenced with sexual favors," Brandon interjected then hesitated and considered the comment. "Well, maybe I can, but the chances of Lady Brighton and Jacklyn's parents all being murdered is a bit insane."

Regan appeared to sink into thought. "Well--"

All eyes were suddenly on Regan.

He shifted uncomfortably. "There's a lot of money here," Regan blurted out. "People kill people for, like, twenty bucks. What would they do for, like, two hundred million?"

"I'm sorry I brought it up," Simon informed them and shifted uncomfortably. "I'm just trying to help a few lonely spirits find peace. Forget I said anything."

"You can always talk to me," Leanne insisted and smiled sweetly. "I'll listen."

"I don't believe in ghosts, I don't believe you see ghosts, and I certainly don't believe they told you they were murdered," Brandon snapped.

Simon jerked, looked away, and placed his hand to his mouth. "Oh, boy--"

"What is it?" Leanne gasped.

Simon shook his head and hid what appeared to be something between a smile and a cringe. Everyone stared at him. The patio lights flickered and a sharp wind blew past them. Several specs of light seemed to travel within the wind. Regan cried out and scrambled from the hot tub. The wind whipped past them and formed into a small tornado. Regan ran for the patio, stopped near the kitchen door, and turned to watch from a safe distance. Jacklyn, Leanne, and Brandon jumped out of the hot tub and looked around with concern. Simon remained comfortably seated and smirked slyly.

Chapter Twenty-four

Later that night. The game room was in a disastrous state with glasses and bottles scattered about, indicating the men had a good time. Rock music blared from the modern jukebox in the back corner. Rick lay half off the sofa creeping closer to the floor, obviously out cold. Not far from the construction worker was Derek, who was passed out on the floor. Ellis and Hyland casually leaned against the pool table with their drinks in their right hand and their chins in their left while staring at the bar in curious silence.

After having changed into dry clothes after their hot tub party, Jacklyn and Regan entered the lounge to check on the others. They stopped within the doorway and were stunned to see Danika dancing seductively on top of the bar in only her red, lacy panties and high heels. Although she was obviously drunk, it wasn't reflective of her slow and sensual dance moves.

"Oh, shit. Dude, I can't go in there," Regan gasped with shock. "She's, like, naked and stuff."

Jacklyn groaned and pulled him across the room toward the pool table and the others. She glared at Ellis and Hyland, who silently studied the dancing woman as if she were an art exhibit.

"You two should be ashamed," Jacklyn scolded the men.

"If a beautiful woman wants to take her clothes off and dance on the bar, who am I to stop her?" Hyland announced without taking his eyes off the half-naked woman.

Jacklyn approached the bar and tapped Danika's leg. Without even looking, Danika lowered herself as if expecting money to be placed in her panties. Ellis quickly searched his pockets. Hyland casually handed him a dollar bill.

"Danika, show's over," Jacklyn announced.

Danika stopped dancing and made a drunken effort to get off the bar. Hyland and Ellis booed Jacklyn as she helped Danika from the bar and kept the giggling woman from falling.

"Oopsy," Danika giggled.

"Yes, oopsy," Jacklyn muttered while smirking, mildly irritated.

Regan handed Danika's dress to Jacklyn without getting too close to the naked woman. Jacklyn snatched the dress, disappointed in Regan's boyish innocence. She then helped Danika slip into her dress while she clung to her and giggled.

"I'll help her to her room," Jacklyn informed Regan then nodded to her uncle and Ellis. "See if you can get them to their rooms."

Jacklyn helped the drunken, swaying woman from the game room.

Danika giggled the entire way. "You're hot," she informed Jacklyn. "Have you ever had woman on woman sex? I could show you."

Hyland, Ellis, and Regan stared after them with looks of surprise and their mouths hanging open.

Regan gasped, "Dude--"

"Not in this case," Ellis muttered.

Chapter Twenty-five

Once Jacklyn had seen Danika safely to her room, she entered the kitchen from the back stairs and ran into Brandon, who had changed from his swimsuit into his casual clothes.

"Are the others still partying in the game room?" Brandon asked. "It's getting late."

"Unfortunately, the game room looks more like a frat party," she replied with a groan. "My uncle and Ellis were the last men standing. I was hoping Regan would have convinced them to go to bed before they passed out along with the others."

"As if either of them are going to listen to Regan," Brandon teased. "Regan's more of a, well, monkey see monkey do."

"I'm sure he's managing just fine," Jacklyn informed him. "You don't give Regan enough credit."

Brandon raised his brows. "Have you met Regan?"

She groaned and shook her head. "He could probably use our help with my uncle," she announced. "He's pretty damned stubborn."

Jacklyn and Brandon left the kitchen and headed down the hall to the game room. They entered the game room and immediately stopped within the doorway. Regan had a drink in his hand and drunkenly sang show tunes with Ellis and Hyland.

Brandon shook his head and cast a look at Jacklyn. "I'm having serious doubts about you putting Regan in charge."

"I was only gone thirty minutes," Jacklyn proclaimed. "How did they corrupt him that fast?"

As they approached the three drunken men at the bar, Regan waved them over and put his arm over Brandon's shoulder, leaning heavily on him.

"I love you, man!"

"Yeah, I love you too," Brandon announced, "but guess what?"

Regan appeared excited and stood straight. "What?"

"It's time for bed," Brandon informed him. "Why don't you walk back with me? You can make sure I don't steal any pastries."

Jacklyn paused by her Uncle Hyland. He smiled drunkenly and hugged her. "There's my girl!" he proclaimed cheerfully. "Where were you all night? We missed you!"

"There was dancing," Ellis informed her.

"We hung out on the patio," she replied.

Regan pulled away from Brandon and stumbled back to the bar to join Jacklyn and Hyland. Brandon once again attempted to collect him.

"We were in the hot tub," Regan announced and practically collapsed on the bar. "Leanne wore her thong bikini."

Brandon attempted to collect Regan, but he wasn't making it easy.

Ellis sank deep into thought, maintaining a serious look. "Yes, I like that bikini."

"Come along, Regan," Brandon announced and attempted to guide him away from the bar.

"And we were talking about all kinds of stuff, like--" Regan began.

Brandon was obviously concerned about what would next come from the cook's mouth. "Regan, Leanne is raiding the pastries," he suddenly cried out. "Stop her!"

Regan appeared horrified and drunkenly ran from the room. Brandon sighed with relief.

"Come on, Major," Jacklyn announced. "Time for bed."

"Party pooper," he scoffed.

Brandon approached Ellis, who was now slumped on the bar while studying the red, lacy bra in his hand.

"Come on, Ellis. I'll walk you to your room," Brandon informed him.

"No, I've decided I'm going to drink myself sober," Ellis insisted.

"Leanne might still be on the patio in her bikini," Brandon informed him.

He hesitated a moment. "Maybe I could use some fresh air," Ellis announced then stood and handed Brandon the bra.

Regan appeared in the game room doorway with an annoyed look. "Leanne wasn't stealing my pastries. You tricked me!"

Jacklyn released Hyland and hurried to Regan. "Come on, Regan. Bedtime."

Regan placed his arm over her shoulder and leaned on her. "Are you going to, like, kiss me again?" he asked in a giddy tone. "Because I have to warn you, your uncle is right there."

"She kissed you?" Hyland barked.

"Don't worry," Ellis casually announced and waved him off. "She kissed me too."

Regan then chuckled. "With an occasional happy ending."

Jacklyn gasped in horror at the comment.

Hyland appeared to immediately sober and pointed at each man in the room. "Okay, someone needs to be hit."

Regan and Ellis pointed at Brandon. Brandon looked at the bra in his hand and quickly tossed it aside.

"Okay, everyone out. Brandon and I are going to have a little talk," Hyland boldly announced then eyed Brandon. "Pour us some drinks."

Brandon turned to Jacklyn and gave her a serious look. "No matter what he says tomorrow, it wasn't an accident."

Jacklyn attempted a smile and left the room with Regan and Ellis. Brandon poured each of them a weak drink.

Hyland sat at the bar and stared at his glass in a moderately sedate manner. "You know I love my niece as if she were my own daughter."

"Yes, I do. I understand."

He glared at Brandon. "Don't talk--listen."

Brandon poured himself a shot and drank the entire contents in one swallow.

Hyland added more vodka to his drink. "Losing her parents when she was only fifteen nearly destroyed her," he announced, "but if she knew her parents were murdered, it'd kill her."

Brandon stared at Hyland with surprise and possible horror. "Murdered? But I thought--?"

"Yeah, it looked like a car accident, but I had some people conduct an unofficial, unauthorized investigation," Hyland informed him. "Fragments found in my brother-in-law's skull didn't come from road debris." Hyland aimed his finger like a gun. "The trajectory was perfectly straight." He cast a look at Brandon. "Their findings indicated small stones had been encased in a shotgun shell and fired into the car at close range."

Brandon poured another shot and drank it in one gulp. He focused his attention on Hyland. "Was there ever an official investigation?"

"No, it was too late," he replied. "I hired the best private detective money could buy, but he vanished after the check cleared." He drew a deep breath and held it a moment. "After Mara got sick, I realized that obsessing just made everyone unhappy. As long as Jacklyn believed it was an accident, she had closure."

"So why are you telling me?"

"Because someone attacked me on my own island," Hyland announced firmly while staring at Brandon. "If there's some crazy connection between what happened, I may unknowingly involve Jacklyn." His look was serious. "If you know the truth, you can keep her safe."

Brandon drank another shot then sank into thought. A curious look suddenly crossed his face. "When did that detective disappear?"

"Nine years ago. In October--"

"The dead guy in the crypt," Brandon gasped.

Hyland stared at Brandon with a look of surprise. "It's conceivable the detective showed up at the party," he announced then shook his head. "He may have been following a lead of some sort and had a run-in with my sister's killer." He shook his head in amazement. "You just found motive for a nine-year-old murder." He grinned proudly. "Not too shabby for a straight interior decorator."

Brandon frowned at the comment. "I wish you'd stop saying that."

Hyland grabbed two shot glasses and filled them. "Now if you can figure out who hit me in the dungeon, I'd feel better."

"I know someone who might be able to help," Brandon remarked then frowned, "but first I have to apologize to the creepy, little fuck."

"I'm not sure what you just said, but it sounded good," Hyland announced while chuckling then raised his shot glass. "To the creepy, little fuck!"

Chapter Twenty-six

Regan was unconscious and slumped over the kitchen table with a cannoli clutched in his hand. Jacklyn followed Ellis as he stumbled across the kitchen to the back door. He looked outside toward the hot tub area with his hands and nose pressed against the glass. She wasn't sure how long the happy, drunken butler stood pressed against the glass door spying on Leanne and Simon, but at least it kept him occupied and out of trouble. He finally groaned and appeared disappointed at what he must have seen.

"Ah, no thong," he pouted then staggered back to the counter.

"We should get you to bed before you pass out," she gently insisted.

"I'm going to make tea," Ellis casually informed her. "Would you like some?"

Jacklyn groaned with defeat. "Sure."

Ellis prepared the kettle with some unsteadiness. "I know it may seem like I'm drunk, but if called upon, my cat-like reflexes will kick in."

As he reached into the cupboard, a mug fell from his fingers and shattered on the floor.

Regan's head jerked up. "Tornado!" His head fell back down with a thud.

Ellis stared with disappointment at the broken mug on the floor. "Now who the hell did that?"

"I'll get that," Jacklyn insisted, afraid Ellis might cut himself on the broken ceramic, and then cleaned up the pieces of mug.

Ellis located the teabags and removed them from the container. Several teabags flew across the floor while a few pelted Jacklyn.

She eyed Ellis then muttered, "Let's hope your cat-like reflexes aren't called upon anytime soon."

She tossed the broken ceramic mug into the garbage and was about to return for the discarded teabags when Ellis turned to her and extended his hand.

"Dance with me?"

"There's no music," Jacklyn informed him then remembered what Leanne had said about the last time he was drunk and wanted to dance.

"I hear it," Ellis announced then grinned proudly. "It's the waltz."

Despite knowing she was making a mistake, Jacklyn smiled and accepted his hand. Ellis gracefully glided her across the massive kitchen without stumbling. He dipped her back slightly, pulled her up, and then smiled drunkenly as they danced.

"Not half bad for a butler, huh?" he teased.

She stared into his eyes with a strange curiousness as they danced within the kitchen. "I often wondered how you came to work for the major," she remarked. "This job doesn't exactly fit you."

"One of life's mysteries," he teased and chuckled. "I always wanted to get married and have children, but that wasn't meant to be." He stared back at her and smiled. "If I had a daughter, she'd be like you."

"Why do I get the feeling that's not a compliment?" she muttered.

"Because you're a real pain in the ass," Ellis remarked then grinned slyly, "but I'd never change you. I love you the way you are."

"That's very sweet," she replied then stopped dancing and hugged him.

He clung to her a moment then caressed her back. "But you're not my daughter," he announced with a sigh near her ear. "I'm very drunk, and I'm thinking some wildly inappropriate thoughts."

"Yes," Jacklyn replied dryly. "That would explain your hand on my ass."

Ellis released her, offered a sly grin, and moved away. The kitchen door opened to reveal Brandon and Hyland hanging on each other for support while laughing.

"Honey, I'm home," Brandon cried out. "What's for dinner?" Brandon drunkenly stumbled across the kitchen and into Ellis on his way to Jacklyn. He kissed him playfully on the cheek and laughed. "Oh, babe, you need a shave." He then stumbled to Jacklyn and threw his arms around her, knocking her against the island counter. "Guess what?"

She stared at him and raised her brows with disapproval. "Uh, you're drunk?"

"I just won you in a game of pool," he announced cheerfully while grinning.

She stared at him with some surprise then smirked. "Huh? That's too bad," she remarked. "I just lost you to Ellis in a poker game."

Brandon stared at her with a puzzled look. "Hmm. Not sure how we work that out," he remarked then grinned. "But the major is okay with whatever we do. Isn't that great?"

"Yes, that's great," she replied, "but you were supposed to help sober him; not get silly with him."

He waved her off. "I'm good," Brandon replied casually. "And since there's two of you that makes it a threesome."

Jacklyn groaned and rolled her eyes. "Oh, boy--"

Brandon released her, took the cannoli from Regan's hand, and ate it.

Ellis stood nearby and shook his head with disapproval. "Inexcusable behavior," he muttered. "Some people shouldn't drink."

Jacklyn eyed her uncle. "I'm taking Brandon to his room," she announced. "When I get back, it's off to bed with you."

Hyland chuckled and saluted her.

Chapter Twenty-seven

Jacklyn helped Brandon into his room within the servant's wing of the main house. She didn't bother turning on the lights since she could see his bed clearly from the hallway light. She relied solely on his ability to find his own room since she didn't have a clue which room was his. She pulled down the covers for him and attempted to assist him into bed when he pulled her down with him. She landed on top of him and struggled to get back up while he did his best to keep her on the bed with him. He appeared disappointed when she finally pulled herself off him. She straightened and removed his shoes for his comfort.

"So you really just intended to tuck me in and nothing else?" he teased.

"I think when a man and woman become intimate for the first time, it should be memorable," she informed him. "A drunken encounter is not what I had in mind."

He made himself comfortable on the bed while watching her then smiled timidly. "I was only half serious," he informed her. "I want it to be special too. Leastwise, I'd like to be able to remember it."

She pulled the covers over him. He struggled to prop himself up on his elbow while facing her.

"Are you mad?"

Jacklyn managed a smile and snorted a laugh. "No, I'm not mad," she replied. "Just tired."

"I didn't intend to drink tonight," he informed her. "It's just when your uncle said--" He suddenly hesitated while staring at her.

"Said what?"

Brandon smiled warmly and shook his head. "Just guy stuff," he replied. "Probably not appropriate to repeat in mixed company either."

"Yes, that sounds like something my uncle would say," Jacklyn teased.

"Are you going to kiss me goodnight?" he asked while grinning boyishly.

Jacklyn laughed softly then leaned down and kissed him quickly on the lips. He attempted to prolong the kiss, but she was quick to pull away.

"Goodnight, Brandon."

He smiled warmly and collapsed onto the bed. "Goodnight, Jacklyn."

§

Jacklyn returned to the kitchen only ten minutes later and found her uncle passed out on the table not far from the unconscious cook. Ellis casually leaned against the counter and sipped his tea.

"I don't think he's making it to his room tonight. Poor bastard is going to have one hell of a hangover," Ellis remarked while shaking his head then eyed Jacklyn with all seriousness. "How was your threesome?"

She rolled her eyes. "Goodnight, Ellis."

Chapter Twenty-eight

Jacklyn slept peacefully in her bed while nestled under the covers. It was nearly four o'clock in the morning when the faint sounds of a dungeon cell creaking echoed throughout her room. Jacklyn stirred then woke. She thought she heard something but wasn't sure what it was. She then heard the faint sound of someone moaning, causing her to jump out of bed. Jacklyn nervously looked around the room. It sounded as if the moans were coming from her room yet from further away.

She followed the sound to the air vent and listened. She could hear the sound more clearly now. Jacklyn hurried from her room, entered the hallway, and approached the hallway vent. She put her ear close to it and listened. She realized that air moving through the vent produced a moaning sound. She was relieved it hadn't been an actual person making that sound, but it was troubling all the same. Simon's door opened to reveal an exhausted Leanne wearing Simon's button shirt.

"Jacklyn, you scared me," the maid gasped then folded her arms across her chest, warding off the cool air within the corridor. "What's with the noise? People are trying to sleep."

Jacklyn eyed her then the room she had exited. "Isn't that Simon's room?"

Leanne tensed slightly and ran her fingers through her mussed hair. "Yeah, long story."

Both women heard the sound again.

"What is that?" Leanne gasped with concern while looking around.

"A breeze blowing through the dungeon," Jacklyn informed her. "The sound is radiating through the vents. There must be an open door."

Leanne's brows sharply raised. "An open door? In the dungeon?" she announced with surprise. "Are you suggesting there's someone in the dungeon at four in the morning?"

"That's exactly what I think," Jacklyn replied as she sank into thought. A stern, determined look crossed her face. "And I'm going to see who's down there playing games."

Leanne appeared alarmed by the comment and darted into the nearby bedroom.

"Simon, wake up," she could be heard within the dark room. "Jacklyn's going into the dungeon *alone*."

§

Twenty minutes later, Jacklyn, Simon, and Leanne followed the strange, non-human moaning sound within the dungeon. They paused on the stone landing above the creepy underground dock and peered at the dark water below. Torches were lit the entire way down the stone steps, indicating someone had been through recently. The water level in the tunnel was down with the tide, and the rotted, sunken boat was now mostly uncovered. Jacklyn gathered all her courage and carefully walked down the steep steps while practically clinging to the wall to keep from feeling dizzy. She paused near the bottom and stared at the now exposed tunnel. A walkway had been uncovered with the receding water. She never even knew that walkway existed since she had made it a habit to avoid the underground dock.

"There's a walkway through the tunnel," Jacklyn announced with surprise to Simon and Leanne, who waited at the top of the steps.

"The steps are wet," he informed her, indicating the wet footprints. "Someone's been here in the last few hours." He considered his comment and immediately straightened while glaring at his friend. "I know you're not thinking about exploring that tunnel tonight. You could run into whoever was down here."

"I'm curious, not stupid," Jacklyn informed him, although she wanted to know who was down there and why. The thought of possibly running into the person responsible for attacking her uncle frightened her. "We'll explore tomorrow after low tide."

Chapter Twenty-nine

The following morning, Jacklyn rode one of her uncle's horses bareback through the woods along several paths before finally ending up on the main beach. Despite riding without a saddle, she rode the horse at a gallop across the beach past Simon's helicopter. It was a beautiful, sunny morning, and the perfect day for a ride around the island. Her uncle owned four Gypsy Vanner horses. They were large, stocky, black and white spotted horses with long manes and tails, and heavily feathered hair hanging down to their hooves.

The gracefulness of a galloping Gypsy Vanner was without compare. The horse had long, powerful strides while arching its thick neck, looking more like a warrior horse prancing into battle. Jacklyn enjoyed the smooth gait of the powerful horse and riding bareback allowed her to feel the horse's muscles beneath her.

"Hey--" a female voice called out interrupting her peaceful morning ride.

Jacklyn slowed the horse and saw Tara in her bikini and sarong as she approached from the path. Jacklyn stopped the horse near Tara.

"I didn't think anyone was up yet," Tara announced cheerfully while pausing before the horse and caressed its large, white nose.

"We went for a ride around the island," Jacklyn replied while patting the horse's thick neck.

"Without a saddle?" she remarked then laughed and shook her head. It was difficult to tell if she was humored or stunned. "You always were a better rider than me. I'm sure I would have fallen off in the first five minutes. That is if I could even get on one of them without a stepladder." Tara was silent a moment then fidgeted and appeared uncomfortable. "About last night; I said some things I shouldn't have. If you and Brandon like each other, then I'm happy for you."

"I appreciate that."

"I mean, there was never anything between us," she informed Jacklyn. "It was mostly just wishful thinking." Tara grimaced slightly. "I've sort of been in a dating slump."

"Maybe you need to concentrate on making yourself happy without a man in the mix," Jacklyn informed her. "There's nothing wrong with spending quality time with yourself."

"Sadly--I've been doing that for a few months now," Tara explained then sighed. "I prefer the company of men over my own. Honestly, I miss the sex too." She then smiled more cheerfully. "If you're heading back, tell Danika I'll be sunbathing here on the beach for a couple of hours."

"Sure, I'll tell her," Jacklyn replied then laughed. "Happy tanning."

Tara smiled slyly and removed her top exposing her full, round breasts. "Definitely."

Chapter Thirty

Regan, Hyland, Brandon, Rick, and Derek sat at the kitchen table with their heads in their hands while silently suffering from their hangovers. Jacklyn entered the kitchen from the patio entrance and immediately eyed the party of five. Ellis stood before the main counter while cheerfully making waffles and smiled at her.

"Good morning, Jacklyn," Ellis announced. "I'm making waffles. Would you like some?"

"Thanks, but I already had a cannoli for breakfast," she replied.

Regan groaned while holding his pounding head. "No, not the cannoli."

Jacklyn approached Ellis at the main counter and nodded toward the men slumped over the table. "Why aren't you over there suffering with the rest of the party animals?"

"I don't get hangovers," he replied.

"Do you remember last night?"

"I remember someone dancing," he remarked, although he seemed uncertain of the details.

"That was Danika, dude," Regan announced. "She liked danced naked on the bar then tried to get it on with Jacklyn."

Brandon lifted his eyes with little other movement. "Where was I during this?"

"I don't know, man," Regan replied. "I just remember, like, the dancing part."

"Wish I remembered that," Rick muttered while clinging to his cup of coffee like a security blanket.

"My girlfriend was dancing naked on the bar in front of everyone?" Derek demanded.

"It's okay, dude," Regan announced enthusiastically. "She owned it."

Derek glared at Regan.

"Who was dancing in the kitchen?" Ellis then asked with some confusion.

"That was you and me," Jacklyn teased.

They heard a moan from the table. "Please tell me no one was naked," her uncle muttered.

Brandon approached Jacklyn and Ellis by the coffeepot. He refreshed his coffee and leaned closer to Jacklyn.

"Did I do anything offensive or obscene?" Brandon timidly asked.

"You kissed Ellis," she informed him.

Ellis and Brandon looked at each other with shared horror. Ellis immediately took a sideways step away from Brandon to put some distance between them. He fidgeted while eyeing Brandon then finally sipped his coffee.

Brandon appeared slightly uneasy. "I actually meant toward you," he reiterated.

"After being French kissed by Danika, you were a welcomed relief," Jacklyn remarked.

Ellis suddenly spit out his coffee.

§

Later that afternoon, Jacklyn entered the game room while Ellis and Leanne cleaned up the mess from the frat party.

Leanne appeared curious as she held up the red, lacy bra. "Some party, huh?"

Jacklyn approached Ellis, who collected glasses. "Ellis, I need to talk to you. It's rather important."

Ellis suddenly looked at her and appeared concerned. "Whatever I did last night; I'm sorry, and it'll never happen again," he announced defensively. "I'm not myself when I drink."

"That's the truth," Leanne muttered. "On New Year's, he kissed me and grabbed my ass."

"That never happened," Ellis snapped while eyeing the maid. He then looked back at Jacklyn. "Leanne just likes to annoy me."

"You grabbed my ass on New Year's Eve too," Jacklyn remarked then considered the comment. "And again last night."

Ellis appeared stunned.

"But that's a conversation for another time," Jacklyn continued and turned serious. "Someone was in the tunnels last night."

"In the tunnels?" he suddenly asked with surprise. "Did you tell your uncle?"

"No, I didn't want him storming the dungeon with his guns blazing."

"So you intended to do it yourself instead?" Ellis remarked while raising a brow. "If someone's playing around down there, it could be dangerous. You're not going down there without me."

Chapter Thirty-one

Later that afternoon, Jacklyn, Brandon, Simon, and Ellis carefully walked down the stone steps to the underground dock. Ellis looked from the sunken boat to the exposed walkway through the tunnel. He seemed to study the tunnel and consider everything he'd been told from last night.

"Why would anyone be down here in the middle of the night?" Ellis finally asked.

"If we knew that, we might know why someone wanted to kill Jacklyn's uncle," Simon replied.

"Simon is right," Brandon informed them. "We should see what's at the other end. It could give us some answers."

Brandon led them into the dark and narrow tunnel by the light of his flashlight. The walkway was narrow and remained wet. The rest of the tunnel still contained water, so they had to be careful not to slip from the walkway into the murky water below. Simon and Jacklyn followed

Brandon with their own flashlights while Ellis brought up the rear, mostly shining his flashlight into the water and behind him. Jacklyn cast several looks into the murky water just beyond the walkway. Due to the darkness of the tunnel, the water appeared dark and creepy. She wondered how deep the water was during low tide. The musty smell combined with the relentless dripping sound echoing off the walls was enough to set her on edge throughout the entire journey.

The tunnel finally led to a cave the size of a football field, which was located not far from the ocean. They'd traveled quite a distance underground. To their surprise, they saw a newer model, thirty-six-foot trawler with twin outboard engines anchored within the cave alongside the walkway. All four stared at the ship with bewildered looks.

"Where did that come from?" Brandon asked and glanced at Ellis.

Ellis stared at the ship, marveled at its grandeur, and shook his head. "I've never seen it before," he announced. "It certainly doesn't belong to Hyland. A fine vessel in its own rights but nothing compared with the major's yacht in the boathouse."

"All right then," Brandon announced with a sigh. "Let's check her out."

Brandon approached the boat's rope ladder and climbed up it to the deck.

Ellis turned to Simon and Jacklyn. "You two wait here and keep your eyes on the tunnel."

Both nodded then watched Ellis climb the rope ladder after Brandon. Jacklyn and Simon exchanged concerned looks then nervously looked around the cave while they waited.

Ellis and Brandon walked along the ship's deck and headed into the control room. Naturally, the control room was empty, leaving Brandon scratching his head with limited ideas. Ellis gave a slight nod to the small door near the back. Brandon opened the door and saw the narrow steps leading into the lower cabin. He flipped a nearby light switch, brightening the steps and the area below. He stared down the steps with some uncertainty then drew a deep breath and was about to head down them. The sound of a semiautomatic weapon being cocked startled him. Brandon looked at the gun Ellis held then met the butler's serious gaze.

"I don't like surprises," Ellis informed him.

Brandon drew a deep breath then walked down the steps into the cabin with Ellis following. The cozy cabin contained a bed, built in dresser, closet, living room set, and a large screen television mounted on the wall. Not surprising, they didn't find anyone. Brandon approached the dresser and opened drawers, hoping to find information on the ship's owner. Ellis tapped his foot across the floor in a sweeping motion, catching Brandon's attention.

When they heard a hollow thump, Ellis pushed back the carpet to reveal a trapdoor. Brandon hurried to join him. Ellis straightened and aimed the gun at the trapdoor then signaled Brandon. Brandon frowned, knowing what that look meant, and pulled open the door. They saw a large pile of gold, jewels, and valuable trinkets hidden within the secret compartment.

"Did someone steal that from Hyland?" Brandon asked while glancing at Ellis.

Ellis shook his head without taking his eyes from the gold and jewels. "No, I've never seen that before," he replied then appeared curious. "There had been rumors about buried pirate treasure on the island. Some of that appears to be fourteenth century. Maybe there was more to the rumors."

"We need to call the police," Brandon insisted while straightening.

Ellis turned to face him and offered a serious look. "By the time the police get here, whoever's behind this could be gone," he replied.

"What do you suggest we do?"

Ellis raised his brows and offered a sly grin. "Up for a little nautical adventure?"

"I certainly don't know much about boats," Brandon remarked then eyed Ellis. "Can you captain a ship this size?"

"Of course, I can," Ellis replied almost sounding offended. "We'll dock her somewhere secure on the far side of the island and walk back."

Chapter Thirty-two

After Ellis anchored the boat on the other side of the island, Brandon, Simon, and Jacklyn followed him along a neatly groomed trail in the woods on their hike back to the mansion. The thick woods offered a peaceful trek for the small group. Hoofprints from Jacklyn's ride were still visible on the trail. Considering the long walk, she wished she had one of the horses now. Ellis and Brandon walked a few lengths ahead of Jacklyn and Simon. The two men seemed to be having a serious conversation that Jacklyn was having a difficult time overhearing, despite her effort at eavesdropping.

"For the record, I don't believe in ghosts," Ellis firmly insisted.

Brandon indicated Simon and Jacklyn just behind them. "Tell that to them," he muttered.

"But with what happened to Hyland, I think we should take Simon's prophecy seriously," Ellis added, surprising Brandon.

"So you actually believe ghosts told Simon someone is out to hurt Jacklyn?" Brandon practically demanded loud enough for the others to hear.

"Not so unbelievable, huh?" Simon snapped while raising his brows.

"I didn't say that," Ellis insisted then appeared to sink into his own thoughts. He hesitated then drew a deep breath. "There's the slight possibility someone may have murdered Jacklyn's parents, and though I'll deny ever saying it, I have my suspicions about Lady Brighton's death as well."

All three suddenly stopped and stared at Ellis. They almost couldn't believe what they were hearing. When he realized they had stopped, Ellis turned and looked at them with mild suspicion.

"Why are you staring at me like that?" Ellis suddenly demanded.

"Simon's ghost told him the same thing," Jacklyn informed him. "No one would believe him."

Ellis stared at Simon with surprise. "Your ghost told you Lady Brighton was murdered?"

Simon folded his arms across his chest and glared demandingly at him. "No, *Lady Brighton* told me she was murdered," he replied.

"Ghosts aside," Ellis announced not wanting to give in to the ghost theory, "there's something very bad on the horizon."

"Considering you felt the need to carry a gun, I guess you feel pretty strongly about that," Brandon boldly remarked.

"I believe in stacking the deck in my favor," Ellis easily corrected him.

They continued along the path toward the cemetery, which was just ahead.

"What now?" Brandon asked.

"We call the police then Simon flies Jacklyn somewhere safe," Ellis replied.

"My uncle is the one who was attacked," Jacklyn reminded them. "If anyone is in danger, it's him."

Ellis cast a look at her. "And if someone wants to get to him, they'll use you to do it," he announced. "The major can take care of himself."

"No one's out to get me," Jacklyn replied. "If they were, I'd be dead by now."

"It might not be such a bad idea to take a little vacation," Simon informed her.

Jacklyn glared at Simon. He looked away and immediately silenced.

"Okay, here's the plan," Brandon announced. "Ellis calls the police, Jacklyn and I will find her uncle and tell him what's going on, and Simon flies to the mainland to bring that detective here to investigate."

Simon suddenly fell silent and stared off a moment. It was a look Jacklyn was coming to understand. She stared at him with interest. Simon appeared bewildered, eyed Ellis, and then looked at Jacklyn.

"Lady Brighton says you should stay close to Ellis," Simon informed her.

Ellis suddenly looked at Simon with surprise, as if he said something shocking. Everyone feared an explosion to Simon's insinuation that he was talking with Lady Brighton. Ellis had always been protective of Lady Brighton and her reputation even after her death. His eyes immediately narrowed as if suddenly curious.

"What?" Ellis gasped. "Did she say why?"

Simon was silent a moment as if listening to someone else speak then gave Ellis a puzzled look. "She said 'you are the storm'," Simon remarked then appeared curious and tilted his head. "What does that mean?"

Ellis stared at Simon with the same strange expression and slowly shook his head. "I have no idea."

Despite what he said, his expression told Jacklyn he knew exactly what Lady Brighton's ghost meant. Ellis turned and continued toward the mansion in more of a hurry with Brandon only a length behind. Jacklyn and Simon exchanged curious looks.

"That was weird," Simon remarked.

"Ellis specializes in weird," Jacklyn muttered.

"No," Simon informed her. "When Ellis said he didn't know what she meant by the comment, Lady Brighton laughed. She wanted to rattle Ellis on purpose."

"My Aunt Mara and Ellis had a weird relationship," Jacklyn remarked. "Regan said she was really mad when Uncle Hyland hired Ellis without consulting her first. A few months later, I guess Ellis caught some of the staff stealing, and she changed her opinion about him. She rarely made a decision without him after that."

"Really?"

"I never understood it myself," Jacklyn remarked. "Ellis and I get along, but he gets under my skin a lot. He can be intimidating at times too."

"Probably hanging out with your uncle too much," Simon teased.

"I don't know," Jacklyn remarked as they followed the men at a leisurely pace. "Although not often, I've seen Ellis intimidate my uncle once or twice."

"I find that very hard to believe," Simon announced while snorting a laugh.

"My uncle is an intimidating man," Jacklyn agreed, "but I think Ellis might be a tad psycho. When he gets that look in his eyes, it's time to vacate the premises."

Simon eyed her and smiled. "I've been told I have a psychotic side," he announced almost proudly.

Jacklyn suddenly laughed. "I'll believe that when I see it," she remarked.

"I didn't say I showed that side often," Simon practically pouted. "But I can be intimidating now and again."

Jacklyn playfully patted his chest while they walked. "I'm sure you can," she announced. "Just don't ever say that in front of my uncle. I'm sure he'll take it as a challenge."

Simon suddenly held his breath. "I'll take your advice."

Chapter Thirty-three

Later that afternoon, Hyland played pool with Derek in the game room while Harry hung out at the bar. After a night of heavy drinking, it was surprising he had the stamina or the stomach to start drinking again so early. Undoubtedly, years of practice.

Derek leaned on his pool stick, watched his uncle sink another ball, and shook his head. "You know, I'm good at pool," he remarked then chuckled. "I don't understand how you can be that much better."

"In the military, there were always plenty of men looking to part you from your money," Hyland remarked then straightened and gave serious consideration to the comment. "Women too, but they were a different breed altogether."

Hyland sank another shot without trying.

"You never talk much about your military days," Derek remarked.

"Most of it is considered classified," Hyland replied. "I wouldn't want to have to kill you."

Derek laughed, finding the comment amusing.

Hyland straightened and gave him a stern look. "Did I say something funny?"

Derek's look turned serious. "You're a scary man, Uncle Hyland."

Hyland sank another ball then straightened and grinned. "I believe you lose again," he announced. "That's four in a row. Pay up."

"You're brutal, Uncle Hyland," Derek remarked then chuckled. "Thankfully, you're not greedy."

Derek placed a dollar on the table. Hyland laughed and collected his money as Derek left. Harry approached the table and racked the pool balls.

"Care to raise the stakes to a hefty five dollars a game?" Harry asked while chuckling.

"I don't play high stakes," Hyland informed him then fell silent while staring at Harry, who didn't bother looking at him while racking the balls. "I'm a little disturbed by what Tara said last night."

"She says stupid things when she drinks," Harry replied with little concern. "We all do."

"I don't know. She seemed convinced you'd inherit the island after my death," Hyland remarked and eyed his brother-in-law. "The will stands. Half the money goes to Derek and Tara, and the other half and the island goes to Jacklyn."

Harry avoided looking at Hyland while removing the triangle from the balls. "I'm aware of the will," he remarked. "A bit heavy in Jacklyn's favor, considering the estate belonged to Mara before you'd met her." He finally straightened and glanced at Hyland while attempting a smile that came off more like a sneer. "It seems odd that

Jacklyn, who's not blood relation to the Brighton family, gets more than Mara's own niece and nephew."

"It was Mara's decision," Hyland responded without emotion. "Despite the fact that you'd spent your entire fortune on *whatever*, Mara made sure Tara and Derek had everything they needed. She was more than generous with them and you."

"That was my family's fortune," Harry snarled in anger. "You just married into it."

Hyland set down his pool stick and sneered. "And there it is! You got your fair share. Just because you blew your share of the family fortune, that doesn't mean you're entitled to Mara's half," Hyland launched back. "And whether you feel I deserve it or not, as her husband, she left everything to me. This island is Jacklyn's legacy from my wife and me. She was the daughter we never had. Mara didn't have to leave *anything* to your children, but she knew you weren't providing for their future, so she made sure she did. With what they get in the will, Tara and Derek will still have more money than they can possibly spend in their lifetime."

"That was my family's fortune," Harry exploded in anger. "You were just the guy fucking my sister!"

Chapter Thirty-four

Brandon and Jacklyn left Ellis in the kitchen. Simon had continued past the mansion and headed for the path leading to the beach for his helicopter. As Brandon and Jacklyn walked along the grand hallway, they heard the sound of shattering glass from the nearby game room. They entered the game room just in time to witness Hyland punching Harry, who was thrown into the bar and toppled several stools. Harry grabbed a nearly empty bottle and swung at him. Hyland defended the blow with his forearm. The bottle shattered and cut his arm, but he was barely fazed by the injury. He grabbed Harry, slammed him against the bar, and pinned him by his throat.

"Give me an excuse!"

Jacklyn ran for the bar and attempted to push Hyland off Harry. "Stop this! Let him go!"

Hyland glared at Jacklyn, sneered, and roughly released Harry. Harry slowly straightened. Jacklyn led Hyland from the bar and attempted to calm him. Harry grabbed his discarded pool stick and swung for Hyland's turned back. Hyland saw him out of the corner of his eye and leaped for his own pool stick. Jacklyn deflected the blow from Harry's pool stick with her forearm, spun into a roundhouse kick, and struck Harry in the chest. He was thrown backward and again struck the bar. Now armed with his own pool stick, Hyland lunged at Harry, who swung as well.

Jacklyn jumped between the two men and caught their pool sticks, one in each hand. She kicked Hyland's arm, forcing him to release his stick, and then kicked Harry in the side, forcing him to release his stick as well. She twirled both sticks in her hands and swung the fat ends at both men, stopping short of their faces. Both men stared at the sticks just inches away from hitting them.

Jacklyn glared at both men with anger. "Either you two end this, or I'm ending it for you!"

Hyland held his hands in the air and backed away. "I bow out gracefully, darling."

Harry clutched his arm and backed away as well. Brandon remained frozen within the doorway, staring with amazement and possible shock. Jacklyn lowered both sticks.

"Now clean up this mess!"

She tossed both sticks to the floor and returned to Brandon within the doorway. She gingerly rubbed her forearm and cringed when she thought neither man was looking.

Brandon continued to stare at her. "Wow--just wow! Are you okay?"

Jacklyn nodded in response while frowning.

Brandon grinned, unable to control his boyish delight. "I'm sorry," he announced while chuckling softly. "I'm just so turned on right now."

Jacklyn glared at him.

He hid his lustful smile and held his hands in the air defensively. "Sorry, don't hurt me."

Jacklyn grabbed him by the face and kissed him aggressively. Brandon jumped with surprise then returned the kiss. She pulled away, took his hand, and pulled him through the doorway.

"Where are we going?" he asked with surprise.

"To my bedroom," she announced gruffly. "I need to release some aggression."

Brandon eagerly picked up his pace to keep up with her.

Chapter Thirty-five

Tara and Danika lay topless on the beach while watching Simon fiddling around within his helicopter. The helicopter began to hum as the engine started. The engine grew louder, and the blades spun. Simon eyed the topless women watching him, who were hopefully far enough away to avoid being pelted with sand kicked up by the rotors. The women smiled and waved. He grinned, enjoying the view, and waved back.

The helicopter lifted off the beach and headed for the ocean. Simon fiddled with some switches while flying close to the crystal blue water and the amazing scenery. He heard faint, whispering voices all around him. One female voice, in particular, caught his attention. He attempted to concentrate on his flying while the voices whispered loudly in his head.

"Oh, this is not a good time for this," he announced and attempted to concentrate on his flying.

An image flashed in his head. *A lady dressed in a gypsy woman costume wearing a feathery, decorative mask aggressively kissed a man dressed like Al Capone. He pinned her against the inner crypt wall near the door and firmly ran his hands along her body while she moaned with pleasure. He unzipped her dress and let it fall to the floor. Al Capone picked up the woman now only wearing her black, lacy panties while she clung to him with her legs wrapped around his hips. He set her on top of the marble crypt and moved partially on top of her without missing a beat. She moaned her intent. He moved off her and slipped her out of her sexy underwear. She writhed around the marble crypt while awaiting her mob boss lover.*

Al Capone slipped out of his suspenders and unbuttoned his pants. The gypsy woman looked up with anticipation. To her surprise, she saw a man dressed in a black, western undertaker costume appear behind Al Capone. She gasped with surprise and immediately sat up while covering her exposed breasts. Al Capone spun around to see what caught her attention.

The man dressed as a western undertaker, complete with black hat and mask, ran a fourteen-inch dagger through Al Capone's mid-section. He gasped, attempted to cry out, but only spit up blood. The gypsy woman screamed and leaped off the crypt. The western undertaker attempted to catch her, but she was already running through the crypt door.

The naked woman ran across the dimly lit garden while screaming and attempted to make it to the noisy, well-lit ballroom. With the ballroom doors closed on the cool night, no one seemed to hear her screams. The western undertaker was directly on her heels and gaining fast. She bolted for the kitchen door but passed it in fear of stopping with the killer directly behind her. She saw the partially open door to the south wing and darted inside. She closed the door and ran from the empty sunroom into the dark corridor. She heard the sunroom door crash open. She darted into the next room.

The conservatory was dark enough for her to find a hiding place. She slipped along the wall and found a dark corner alongside the fireplace. The bookcase moved, surprising her. She saw the killer enter the room, but it was too dark for him to see her. He removed a flashlight and shined it around the room. She braced her body against the bookcase alongside the fireplace. The bookcase moved further. She discovered the dark opening and slipped inside, gently closing the secret passageway behind her.

The naked woman entered the secret parlor room and closed the door behind her. She nervously looked around the nearly dark parlor. As she surveyed the room, thinking she was safe, the passageway suddenly opened. The woman spun around with surprise as the killer approached her with the bloodstained dagger. He leaped for her and knocked her against the nearby wall. She flailed her arms around wildly and pulled the mask from his face. Horror filled her eyes.

Simon stared out the helicopter windshield with a look of horror on his face. "Oh, shit," he cried out. "I have to warn them!"

He turned the helicopter and headed back to the beach. He hadn't gotten too far, so the beach was just up ahead. The ghostly image of Lady Brighton appeared in the co-pilot's seat. Even as a ghost, Mara was a captivating woman. She still wore the long, white dress she was both married and buried within. Simon eyed her several times and noted her terrified expression.

"What's wrong?" he asked with concern.

"You're next," Lady Brighton gasped.

Simon shot looks out the window then at his ghostly co-pilot. "What?"

The helicopter sputtered, alarming him. Simon fiddled with switches as the stick vibrated in his hand.

"They won't let you leave. They want what you took from them, and they're going to use your death to break Jacklyn," Lady Brighton cried out. She watched as he attempted to lower the helicopter and make it to the beach. "You won't be able to land. You'll never make it. There's no time!"

The engine began to expel large amounts of smoke. Simon appeared horrified then looked back at Lady Brighton's frightened expression. From across the beach, Tara and Danika watched the sputtering helicopter in the near distance. It was suddenly engulfed in flames and spun wildly before crashing onto a large reef, exploding on impact. The entire beach vibrated from the explosion. Both women screamed, grabbed their clothes, and ran for the path.

Chapter Thirty-six

Jacklyn paced the kitchen while Leanne and Regan attempted to calm her. Tara and Danika sat at the table huddled over cups of hot tea. Both women were equally traumatized by what they witnessed. Ellis stood near the counter with a hard to read expression and watched Jacklyn pace. The kitchen door opened to reveal Brandon, Hyland, and Rick. Jacklyn ran to Brandon and looked into his eyes. He avoided her gaze. She then looked at her uncle, who frowned.

"We searched the entire area and what was left of the wreckage," Hyland gently informed her then shook his head. "We couldn't find him."

Brandon pulled Jacklyn into his arms and held her. She trembled then sobbed softly. Hyland kissed her on the head then approached Ellis, who watched Jacklyn with the same glazed over stare.

"What's the status on the police?" Hyland asked with a curious look.

"The line to the mainland is dead," Ellis muttered, lacking enthusiasm.

"What about the radio?" Rick suddenly demanded and approached them.

"It's, like, trashed, dude," Regan informed him. "Someone doesn't want us calling for help."

Danika suddenly looked up from her tea mug. "You mean we're trapped here?"

"There's no need for concern. We still have the yacht in the boathouse," Hyland replied. "We'll take a nice, little cruise to the mainland." He looked at Ellis. "Find Harry and Derek and tell them we're meeting on the dock in fifteen minutes--no excuses."

Ellis left the kitchen to alert the others while Hyland turned to Rick.

"Gather your men," Hyland informed him.

Rick drew a deep breath and shook his head. "There's no need to go off half-cocked, Hyland," he announced. "It was a tragic accident."

"Communication has been cut off," Hyland insisted. "I'm not so sure what happened to Simon was an accident. We should leave together."

"My men and I will be fine," Rick informed him. "You do what you need to do to feel safe. My men are construction workers. They'd love the opportunity to beat the crap out of someone. We'll keep the place safe until you can send the authorities and straighten out the communications issue."

"I don't know, Rick," Hyland announced while shaking his head.

"We'll be fine," Rick replied. "Trust me."

A few minutes later, Hyland led the small group to the main beach just before the dock and boathouse. Regan and Ellis brought up the rear with Harry dragging his feet in front of them.

"This is paranoid," Harry scoffed. "Our boat captain will be coming back for us in two days. We're not completely cut off. We don't all have to go for the police."

"Chill, dude," Regan announced with some irritation. "Like, enjoy the boat ride."

"I'll bring the yacht out of the boathouse to the dock," Hyland informed them then headed for the dock and boathouse.

Everyone waited on the beach not far from the dock as Hyland approached the door to the large boathouse. Jacklyn couldn't help but stare at the charred reef as helicopter debris floated to shore. She suddenly felt chilled and swore she felt cold fingers touching her shoulder. Jacklyn suddenly shivered then looked at Hyland as he opened the boathouse door. The boathouse suddenly exploded, and her uncle was thrown backward from the force and into the water. Everyone screamed as the beach vibrated beneath their feet.

"Hyland!" Jacklyn cried out.

Brandon ran across the dock and, without hesitation, dove into the water. Jacklyn attempted to run for the dock after him. Ellis caught her by the arm and stopped her from following. Brandon surfaced in the water and looked around, but he couldn't seem to find the missing man. There was a glowing light dancing on the water along with the sweet smell of perfume. When he looked closer at the light, he saw Hyland just beneath the surface of the clear water.

Brandon swam toward the glowing light, dove under the water, and surfaced a moment later with Hyland. He swam for shore with the unconscious man in tow. Everyone ran to the surf to help pull him out. Regan and Ellis dragged Hyland onto the sand. Ellis checked his breathing as Jacklyn kneeled alongside her uncle unable to do little more than stare helplessly.

"He's not breathing," Ellis gasped then immediately performed CPR.

Jacklyn sobbed while holding her uncle's slightly burnt hand as she felt for a pulse. She stared at her uncle with horror.

"He doesn't have a pulse," she gasped.

"It's okay, Jacklyn," Ellis calmly reassured her and continued with chest compressions.

Everyone watched in silence and horror.

"Breathe for me you stubborn son-of-a-bitch," Ellis muttered under his breath.

As if on command, Hyland coughed and spit up water. Jacklyn cried out with relief and held him.

Regan glared at Harry and raised demanding brows. "Who's paranoid now?"

Chapter Thirty-seven

Hyland sat at the kitchen table while Leanne cleaned the burn on his hand. He was lucky his injuries weren't severe. He only had a few minor burns and some scratches. Jacklyn, Brandon, and Ellis stood in a small huddle near the counter and talked quietly among themselves. The others had returned to the game room for a few drinks after their ordeal.

"We *need* to get the other boat," Brandon insisted.

"They could be waiting for that," Ellis remarked in a low, calm tone while leaning his back against the counter. "We'd be ambushed before we set foot on deck."

"Give me a gun," Jacklyn snarled softly while glaring at Ellis. "I want that bastard." She could feel her entire body twitching with anxiety.

Regan entered the kitchen and joined them by the counter. "The others are in the game room settling their nerves," he announced. "What now?"

Jacklyn maintained her demanding glare directed at Ellis. "Give me a gun," she again snarled.

Hyland looked up from the table and glared at the conspirators in the corner. "Give her a gun over my dead body!"

"He has, like, really good hearing," Regan informed them.

"I'll go for the boat," Brandon announced.

"Not without me," Jacklyn snapped.

"If you people don't stop conspiring, I'm coming over there," Hyland launched with anger.

Brandon finally turned to face Hyland over the nearby island counter. "Someone has to go for that boat. If the others are together, I won't be followed," he announced. "No one knows where we anchored it, so no one's tampered with it. We need to get help."

"No, *you* need help," Hyland growled then removed his Bowie knife from his boot and thrust it into the table without taking his eyes off Brandon. "I need revenge. Whoever is doing this knows you took their treasure, and they want it back." He eyed the others. "They rigged Simon's helicopter and the boathouse then cut all communication. They're just sitting back and waiting for you to screw up."

"You're giving this guy too much credit for ingenuity," Brandon informed him. "We need that boat."

"No, what we need is a counterattack," Hyland snarled loudly in anger.

Regan eyed Brandon and shook his head. "Dude, you're wasting your breath," he announced. "You weren't here for the great, summer rat invasion. When he's like this, it's easier just to stay out of his way."

"And what are we supposed to do?" Leanne suddenly demanded. "Ellis, Regan, and I aren't trained killers; we're the hired help. We clean, cook--" She indicated Ellis with a nod. "--and annoy. What do we do while you're waging your war?"

"I don't know about you dudes," Regan announced, "but I intend to bend over and kiss my ass goodbye."

"Can the radio be fixed?" Jacklyn asked.

"Derek has a knack for gizmos," Regan remarked. "Maybe he can fix it."

Hyland stood with some discomfort. "No one goes anywhere alone," he announced in a gruff tone. "Regan, you and Leanne find Derek and see if he can fix the radio." He then turned to his faithful butler. "Ellis, you and Jacklyn wait for me in the study. Do *not* give her a gun. If she does something stupid, it's your ass, understood?"

"Yes, Major."

"I think I should go with Jacklyn," Brandon announced while indicating Jacklyn.

Hyland glared at Brandon and pointed demandingly. "You're with me."

Chapter Thirty-eight

Brandon studied a large portrait of Mara above the fireplace within the master bedroom while Hyland painfully changed into dry clothes. The master bedroom was roughly the size of a luxury suite at some posh five-star hotel. The tall king-sized bed contained thick posts extending upward to a tall canopy. The comforter and furnishings had a woman's touch, indicating he hadn't changed anything since his wife died. Hyland finished buttoning his shirt and eyed Brandon as he studied the portrait.

"Beautiful, wasn't she?" he asked with a grin.

"Hmm?" Brandon announced, breaking out of his trance then looked back at Lady Brighton's portrait. "Oh, yes, very." He smelled a familiar scent in the air and appeared bewildered while giving Hyland a strange look. "Do you smell perfume?"

"Yeah, her favorite is on her dressing table," Hyland announced with a chuckle. "Sometimes when I'm missing her, I'll give her perfume bottle a little spritz and pretend she's here."

Brandon stared at the painting and appeared even more bewildered. A light glistened only a few inches from his face and seemed to be glowing from the woman's portrait. The strange light appeared similar to what he had seen within the water, which had indicated the location of Hyland's unconscious body.

"Is something wrong?"

Brandon stared at the portrait with possible disbelief. "Just something Simon said," he remarked. "The son-of-a-bitch may have been right."

"About what? Ghosts again?"

"He insisted he was talking to Lady Brighton's ghost," Brandon reluctantly informed him. "Something he said rattled Ellis. I think he believed him."

"Ellis is a little too smart to fall for that sort of bullshit," Hyland remarked while grinning, apparently humored at the thought.

"When I dove into the water for you, I saw a flickering light," Brandon informed him. "That's how I was able to see you beneath the water." He fidgeted slightly. "What's really strange is that I'd swear I smelled your wife's perfume."

Hyland glared at him and shook his head in disbelief. "Don't you think if the woman I loved were haunting these halls, I'd be the first to feel her presence?" he announced with some annoyance.

Brandon sank into thought. "What was it Simon said?" It then came to him. "Despite what you think, the dead *can* hurt the living."

Hyland stared at Brandon a moment in silence then shook his head. "I pushed you too hard, didn't I?" he announced with a sigh. "Your little neurons are misfiring." Hyland straightened proudly. "We need to get back to reality here, Brandon. We need to deal with what we do know. We need to fight back."

Hyland approached the bookcase and popped it away from the wall to reveal a collection of weapons within a hidden compartment. Brandon approached and stared at the collection with some surprise.

"The element of surprise is your best friend," Hyland remarked then revealed a stun gun. "This is a stun gun. It's tiny but effective, especially when applied to delicate, private areas." Hyland handed it to Brandon then removed a palm sized gun in a small, strange holster. "This is a two-shot derringer. I'll help you attach this to your arm and show you how to eject it." He gave him a stern, warning look. "Not a lot of stopping power. You have to be relatively close if you intend to stop someone with it."

Brandon eyed the weapon and appeared uncertain about handling it. Hyland handed the tiny pistol to Brandon and then removed a foot long baton.

"This is Little Jimmy," Hyland announced then flicked his wrist allowing the baton to extend to three feet. Brandon jumped with surprise while Hyland grinned. "Little Jimmy is self-explanatory."

Chapter Thirty-nine

Ellis and Jacklyn remained within the study while waiting for the others to return from their assignments. Jacklyn paced before the locked gun cabinet, occasionally eyeing it, while Ellis played with the dart gun and studied the tiny darts.

"I'm not giving you a gun," Ellis announced without looking at her. He then muttered, "You're scary enough without one."

"Just because you're passive--" she snapped.

He cast a glance at her. "I know that look," Ellis announced. "It's the look of revenge coupled with not thinking rationally. That combination gets people killed." Ellis returned to playing with the darts.

Jacklyn moved in front of him, stood uncomfortably close, and glared at him. "Someone murdered my best friend and nearly killed my uncle," she snapped in anger. "I have every right to want them dead."

He stared back into her eyes and showed little emotion. "Leave revenge to those not burdened by guilt," Ellis remarked in a callous tone.

Somehow the docile man's look frightened her. She fidgeted and moved away. Ellis fired the dart gun at the dartboard. It hit dead center. Regan and Leanne hurried into the study.

"Derek couldn't fix the radio," Regan announced. "He said it was, like, totally messed." He raised his brows. "His words were more colorful. When we returned to the game room, everyone was gone."

"What do you mean gone?" Ellis demanded and sat up straight in his chair.

"As in they weren't, like, there," Regan replied. "Derek went to his room to look for Danika."

"What goes on in the minds of some people?" Ellis muttered while shaking his head.

Brandon and Hyland entered the study. Hyland looked refreshed while Brandon appeared distracted as he approached Jacklyn.

"Everything okay?" she asked noting his look.

"Sure, except the part where your uncle did everything but wire me with a vest bomb," Brandon muttered.

"How's that?"

"He strapped so many weapons and booby traps to my body; I'm afraid to sit down in fear of exploding," Brandon informed her while fidgeting.

Jacklyn laughed, humored at the comment. "Oh, really? Did he remember the--" She felt his inner thigh and hesitated as her expression dropped while she stared at him.

"I'm begging you; watch your hands," he announced sternly while seemingly holding his breath.

"He made you wear the thigh holster?"

"Made nothing," he practically cried out. "He put it on me. I'm feeling violated three ways to Sunday."

She stared at him with her mouth hanging open. Her expression immediately turned to anger as she spun to face her uncle.

"Yet I can't have a gun?" she demanded. "How's that fair?"

"Your uncle manhandles me and turns my body into a weapon of mass destruction, and you're upset because you didn't get a gun?" Brandon suddenly asked.

Jacklyn ignored the comment and approached her uncle and Ellis by the open gun cabinet. Ellis handed Hyland several magazines, which he placed in various pants and jacket pockets.

"You're not getting a gun, Jacklyn," her uncle insisted without looking at her.

Hyland loaded a semiautomatic and handed it to Regan. Regan accepted the gun and appeared concerned.

"You're giving a gun to Regan?" she demanded while folding her arms across her chest.

"He passed gun safety; you didn't."

Jacklyn glared at Regan.

He shrugged and placed the gun down the back of his pants. "Sorry, dude," he announced to Jacklyn. "I'm not the one who shot Ellis."

Brandon appeared surprised and eyed Ellis.

"The thought of her with a gun to this day gives me a pain in the ass," Ellis muttered.

"And I said I was sorry," Jacklyn scoffed. "That was seven years ago."

"You did shoot him in the ass," Regan casually reminded her. "I'm the one who had to change the dressings every day. Honestly, I haven't exactly forgiven you for that."

Hyland handed Brandon a semiautomatic gun in a shoulder holster.

Brandon groaned and reluctantly took the holster. "Not another one."

"Just put it on, you big baby," Hyland snarled then eyed Ellis and mocked Brandon. "One little thigh holster, and it's the end of the world."

Ellis chuckled and slipped into his own shoulder holster then replaced his jacket. Jacklyn remained annoyed and leaned against the side of the cabinet.

Hyland darted a look at Jacklyn then turned to Ellis while indicating Jacklyn. "Keep an eye on her." He then looked at Regan. "Regan, watch the door."

Regan hurried to the door as Hyland slipped into his own shoulder holster. Ellis locked the cabinet and put the key in his pocket. Jacklyn eyed his pocket. Ellis noted her look, removed the key, and stuck it down the front of his pants. They exchanged sneers.

"Tell me, Ellis, how are you on a horse these days?" Hyland asked.

"Mildly panic-stricken to extremely terrified," Ellis casually replied. "Why?"

"Because you and Jacklyn are going out for a little ride," Hyland announced.

"I can ride," Brandon interjected.

"You're going with me," Hyland informed him.

"I haven't fully recovered from our last outing together," Brandon muttered under his breath.

"We're going for the boat," Hyland replied.

"Then what am I doing?" Jacklyn demanded.

"You and Ellis are the diversion," her uncle replied simply. "Disable the four wheelers and set the other horses free so no one can follow too closely. Brandon and I will slip undetected through the passageway in the dungeon. By the time we get to the exit in the cemetery, you and Ellis will be far from here."

Regan stood by the door and looked back at Hyland. "What should Leanne and I do?"

Hyland opened a drawer, removed several hand radios, and tossed one to Regan and the other to Ellis. "You and Leanne will be on lookout from the third-floor balcony. You see anything; you report in."

Hyland pulled a lever near the gun case. It slid away from the wall to reveal an arsenal of intimidating looking assault rifles. He tossed one to Regan.

Regan caught the rifle and looked at it with wide eyes. "Whoa."

Chapter Forty

Jacklyn had two horses tied in the aisle of the bright, airy barn. The barn contained six box stalls with double doors and mesh dividers between stalls. There was a tack room, a cement wash stall, and a feed room. While she saddled the first two horses with expensive western tack, the other two horses roamed freely about the aisle. Ellis stood by the partially open barn door and kept watch for intruders.

Jacklyn finished saddling the horses and glanced at Ellis. "Ready."

Ellis lifted his hand radio and spoke into it. "We're on our way."

He opened the barn door then approached Jacklyn and the saddled horses. Jacklyn held the reins to his horse. He eyed her then the horse with some apprehension and shook his head.

"Why do I get the feeling that this isn't going to end well?" he muttered.

Ellis struggled to mount the large horse and nervously situated himself in the saddle. Jacklyn easily jumped onto her horse without use of stirrups then chased the two loose horses from the barn. When she looked back, Ellis' horse remained standing in the aisle. Jacklyn rode back to him and chased his horse from the barn while he did little more than cling to the saddle horn. The two loose horses roamed around outside the barn. Jacklyn cracked her reins and yelled. The horses ran for the path with Jacklyn chasing after them. Ellis' horse took off after them with Ellis holding on for his life.

§

Hyland led Brandon along the dimly lit dungeon corridor while holding his assault rifle at the ready. Brandon kept watch behind them to ensure they weren't being followed. They heard faint screams echoing from somewhere within the dungeon. Hyland stopped Brandon and listened. The female screams continued.

"That sounds like Tara," Hyland announced then zeroed in on the location of the screaming. "This way. Stay alert."

As they hurried along the corridor with their weapons firmly in hand, the screaming got louder.

"Help! Anyone!" came Tara's terrified voice.

As the men rounded the corner, they saw Tara and Danika locked inside one of the dungeon cells not far from the adjoining corridor. Both women appeared slightly battered with dried blood streaking their temples, indicating they'd been knocked out before being dragged into the dungeon.

"Thank God!" Tara practically sobbed.

"We didn't think anyone would ever find us," Danika gasped with relief.

Hyland removed a small plastic explosive and placed it on the padlock.

Brandon eyed Hyland while keeping watch on the corridor behind them. "You're scary prepared," he announced.

Hyland grinned and lit the fuse. Both women ran to the back of the cell while Hyland and Brandon took cover. Although it did make one hell of a racket, the lock exploded without much damage to the cell or surrounding area. Both women hurried out of the cell and joined Hyland.

"Who did this?" Hyland asked.

Both women shook their heads while clinging to each other for comfort.

"We went to the bathroom down the hall together for safety like you told us," Tara informed him. "Next thing I knew, we were in that cell."

"I never saw anyone," Danika confessed. "It all happened so fast."

"Follow me," Hyland announced with a stern look. "Keep alert and stay quiet."

Both women nodded. They headed for the connecting corridor and walked in silence for several yards. A shot was heard firing from behind them. Hyland grunted and went down. Without hesitation, Brandon shoved the women into an open cell, moved into the cell doorway, and fired blindly down the corridor. Hyland clutched his bleeding leg and dragged himself into the cell while Brandon continued to fire at nothing, covering the injured man. A shot was fired back, surprising him. Brandon darted inside the cell and to safety. Danika examined Hyland's wound then tore her shirt and tied it around his thigh.

"The bullet didn't hit any major arteries, but you need a doctor," Danika informed him.

"Yeah, that crossed my mind too," Hyland remarked while cringing in pain.

"Suggestions?" Brandon asked.

"I have one or two," Hyland replied.

Hyland removed several magazines and lined them on the floor near him. Brandon ejected the empty magazine from his gun and clumsily replaced it.

"I'll hold them off long enough for you and the women to get away," Hyland announced then removed a canister from his pocket.

"Is that a grenade?" Tara suddenly gasped while staring at the can with horror.

"No, my dear. A grenade would bring the entire dungeon down," he informed her. "This is tear gas. I'm going to roll this down the corridor. You and Danika are going to run in the opposite direction for the stairs. Do you know the way?"

Tara nodded.

Hyland handed Tara the hand radio then gave her a stern look. "Once you're safely upstairs, radio for Regan. He'll help you." He then eyed Brandon. "You're going for the boat. The left corridor will take you to the cemetery."

"What about you?" Brandon asked.

"You just worry about the boat," Hyland insisted. "I have plenty of tricks up my sleeve. Don't come back for me without the police, understood?"

Brandon frowned his response.

"And under no circumstances is Jacklyn to come down here," he ordered while glaring into his eyes. "I'll hold you and Ellis responsible if she does." He straightened proudly. "Get ready."

Hyland slid closer to the bars while the women stood ready by the cell door. Hyland pulled the pin and rolled the smoking canister down the corridor.

"Go."

The women ran to the right, and Brandon ran to the left as smoke swiftly filled the entire corridor.

Chapter Forty-one

Jacklyn and Ellis rode their horses at a leisurely canter along the wide, smooth wooded trail. The two unsaddled horses strayed behind, finding more interest in the lush grass on either side of the trail than a tour of the island. Ellis and Jacklyn rode quite a distance from the barn before the radio crackled, alerting them to radio chatter.

"Hello! Hello! Regan, Ellis?" Tara's terrified voice called out over the radio. "Are you there?"

Ellis and Jacklyn stopped their horses when they heard Tara's voice on the radio.

"It's Tara," Ellis remarked with confusion and removed the radio so he could hear better.

"Tara?" Jacklyn gasped with surprise. "Where did she get a radio?"

Ellis shook his head and listened without responding to the urgent call. Jacklyn didn't understand why he didn't respond to the distraught woman, but he never did things that made any sense.

"Tara?" Regan's voice crackled over the radio. "Is that you? We were looking for you. Where did you get the radio?"

"I'm with Danika. Someone shot Uncle Hyland," she shouted into the radio while nearly sobbing. "He's trapped in the dungeon and sent us for help."

"Where are you?" Regan was heard asking. "We'll be right there."

"We're in the kitchen," came her terrified response. "Please hurry!"

"We need to go back," Jacklyn informed Ellis with concern while circling her anxious horse.

Ellis looked around, straightened a moment in the saddle, and carefully considered their next move. She stared at him with surprise when he didn't immediately agree with her.

"Ellis, he needs us."

He ignored her, held the radio to his mouth, and finally responded to the urgent call. "Regan. Copy?"

"Yeah, did you hear?" Regan announced over the radio sounding out of breath. "We're on our way down the stairs now."

"Regan, under no circumstances are you to go after Hyland," Ellis informed him.

Jacklyn stared at Ellis with her mouth hanging open. "What?" she cried out.

"Seriously?" Regan shouted through the radio almost in unison with Jacklyn.

"Yes, Regan," he launched with mild irritation. "Do as I say!"

"Okay, dude," Regan announced from the other end. "Your call."

Jacklyn swung her horse closer to Ellis with hostility on her face. "You're just going to leave him down there to die?" she demanded. "He's not just your boss. He's your friend!"

"There's nothing Regan and Leanne can do for the major if he's under fire and injured," Ellis informed her while attempting to sound calm. "He'll just take them down with him."

"We can't just leave him there!"

"You're not going after him."

"And I'm sure you'd stop me," she announced while glaring at him, "if you could catch me."

Jacklyn spun her horse and galloped down the trail. Ellis' horse pranced around excitedly while he attempted to control it.

"Son-of-a-bitch," he cursed then sent his horse into a gallop after her.

§

Regan and Leanne hurried down the back stairs quickly and quietly then entered the kitchen. They saw Danika seated at the kitchen table with her arms bound in front of her and duct tape over her mouth. She attempted to scream a warning through the duct tape. Despite their confusion, Regan and Leanne were about to run to assist her when a gun cocked behind them.

"Drop it, Regan," Tara snarled.

Regan cursed, dropped the rifle, and raised his hands. Tara kicked the rifle away from him then removed the handgun from the back of his pants.

"Now, both of you--over there," she announced while waving the handgun.

Regan and Leanne crossed the kitchen and uncertainly sat at the table with Danika while casting looks at Tara. She removed a second hand radio.

"Brandon should be at the cemetery entrance any minute," Tara announced urgently into the hand radio. "He's heading for the boat. Don't let him out of your sight."

"Why are you doing this?" Regan asked.

"Wealth and power, obviously," Tara announced proudly. "It's bad enough Uncle Hyland got my aunt's estate, but I wasn't going to let him have the treasure I found in the dungeon cavern. Ironically, the pirate treasure was real, if you can believe that."

Derek entered the kitchen from the hallway entrance. He was slightly out of breath after his short sprint. Danika appeared horrified and gasped beneath the duct tape over her mouth. He glanced at his bound girlfriend seated at the table and grinned slyly.

"What's wrong, sweetheart?" Derek teased as his smile mocked her. "Feeling a little betrayed? That's what you get for dumping me." He shook his head with disapproval. "And to think, I was actually going to include you in our little venture."

Danika's eyes narrowed as she muffled curse words from beneath the duct tape. He laughed at her then waved her off.

"That's okay. I can afford a dozen more like you." He glanced at Tara. "Tie up those two." Derek then looked around the kitchen and frowned. "We need to move them somewhere less accessible. There are too many entry points. We don't want to end up surrounded." He chuckled at the irony. "At least I learned something from Uncle Hyland."

"Uncle Hyland is as good as dead, isn't he?" Tara demanded with some concern. "You assured me he was as good as dead. If you're so certain, what are you worried about?"

"The major isn't dead until he's really dead," Derek informed her then considered their options. "Jacklyn's our only real threat now, thankfully she trusts you."

"Ellis is with her."

"What's he going to do?" Derek demanded and rolled his eyes. "Talk us to death? You just worry about Jacklyn. Let me worry about the butler."

Chapter Forty-two

A tombstone scraped off its marble base within the cemetery. Brandon poked his head out of the vertical shaft and looked around. When nothing moved, he climbed out of the passageway and closed the entrance behind him. The same glowing light appeared in front of his face and zipped past him.

"Lady Brighton?" he gasped softly with surprise.

Brandon turned to follow the light and saw Anderson standing behind him holding a gun. The glowing ghostly light was attempting to warn him, but he was too slow. Anderson chuckled and took the gun from Brandon's shoulder holster.

"Something funny, Anderson?" Brandon demanded while containing his emotions.

"Dying in a cemetery," Anderson chuckled, "kind of convenient, huh?"

Anderson punched Brandon in the mouth and dropped him to his knees. He laughed and flexed his hand. "You don't know how long I've wanted to do that."

Brandon slowly pulled himself to his feet while dabbing the blood from the corner of his mouth. As he straightened, he rammed the stun gun into Anderson's groin, zapping him. Anderson thrashed and fell to the ground while twitching. Brandon raised an arrogant brow while watching the twitching man.

"About as long as I've wanted to do that."

He dragged Anderson into the nearby crypt, braced the door shut, and ran for the trail in the woods. Moments after he disappeared down the path, Jacklyn rode her horse at a gallop from the opposite trail toward the stables with Ellis only a few lengths behind her. She rode into the cemetery, dismounted as the horse slid to a stop, and ran to the tombstone entrance. Ellis appeared on his horse, dove from the moving animal, and tackled her roughly to the ground. They rolled together several feet with Jacklyn eventually landing on top. She straddled his waist and coiled her fist back prepared to punch him.

Ellis held his hands up defensively. "Jacklyn, listen to me," he announced while attempting to keep her from inflicting pain upon him. "The major always has a plan, and I assure you, you're not part of it. Let him do what he does best."

"I'm through listening to you," Jacklyn growled. "You may not have the balls to do anything about it, but I'm going after him." She glared her intent. "And I'm going to need your gun."

Jacklyn reached for the gun within his shoulder holster. Ellis suddenly grabbed her wrists and flipped her over, reversing their positions. His quick reflexes and ability to overtake her surprised her. Ellis straddled Jacklyn's waist, pinned her wrists to the ground on either side of her head, and hovered over her. The look in his eyes was almost frightening.

"I'm through asking nicely," Ellis snarled with his face only inches from hers. "My job is to keep you alive, and I'll do it by force if I must." His eyebrows raised demandingly. "Are we clear or are we going to have a problem?"

Jacklyn attempted to free herself but was unsuccessful. She finally relaxed beneath him.

"I'm thinking we're going to have a problem," she remarked, "but you seem to have me at a slight disadvantage."

"I can play this game all day," Ellis snarled as his eyes narrowed. "And, honestly, I enjoy clipping your wings."

"I'll bet you do," she muttered while staring into his eyes. "You've given me little choice."

Jacklyn lifted her head and kissed Ellis passionately on the mouth. He tensed with surprise. In one swift motion, she broke his hold, flipped him off her, and jumped to her feet. She took an aggressive karate stance.

Ellis immediately sprang to his feet and faced her. "You really don't play fair, do you?" He gingerly touched his mouth. "You bite too."

"Know your enemies weaknesses and exploit them," Jacklyn announced sternly. "It's not my fault you're sexually repressed." She cocked her head to the side and glared at him. "Now I'm asking you nicely to get out of my way. Or would you like to try and clip my wings again?"

"You want to go through me?" Ellis asked then squinted at her. "Give it your best shot, little girl."

Jacklyn sneered at him. They heard pounding coming from the nearby crypt. Ellis and Jacklyn looked back at the crypt with surprise as the door was broken open. Ellis pulled Jacklyn to the ground behind a large headstone. Both peered out. Anderson stormed from the crypt and grabbed the discarded hand radio. Thankfully, the horses had already returned to the barn, so he wasn't warned of their return.

"Brandon got away," Anderson snarled into the hand radio. "He's heading for the boat. Should I go after him?"

"No, let him bring the boat to us," Derek replied through the radio. "We'll get him on the dock. Go to the library and wait for Jacklyn. We have Regan and the girls with us."

"Okay, I'm on my way," Anderson announced then hurried to the mansion.

As Ellis stared after the dangerous man heading for the back, kitchen entrance, Jacklyn cast a look at him.

"Care to take a rain check on beating the hell out of each other?" Jacklyn asked.

He finally looked at her with a stern, serious look. "You're going to have to trust me if we're going to save them," Ellis informed her.

"Do you have a plan?"

"I always have a plan," Ellis remarked calmly, "and the library has a secret passageway."

Chapter Forty-three

Hyland sat against the cell wall with his gun across his lap while admiring his crudely made plastic explosive attached to a tear gas can. He painfully moved to his knee, lit the fuse, and threw the can down the corridor. Hyland took cover and listened to the metal can rolling along the stone floor.

Ellis and Jacklyn climbed over the balcony wall and silently entered the master bedroom through the glass doors. There was a low rumble, and the entire mansion vibrated from what felt like an explosion within the dungeon.

"What was that?" Jacklyn exclaimed with alarm while looking around.

"That was the major taking care of business," he casually replied.

Ellis continued toward the bookcase near the fireplace. The bookcase opened to expose a dark passageway. He politely extended his hand to the opening. Jacklyn grinned and entered. Ellis shut the bookcase behind him.

§

Smoke and debris rolled along the corridor in a huge ball and into Hyland's dungeon cell. He shielded his face a moment then slowly looked up as the smoke cleared. The dungeon corridor was nearly dark since most of the torches had been extinguished or destroyed. He pulled himself to his feet and limped into the doorway with his rifle aimed. Nothing moved that he could actually see, but there was too much smoke to see more than a few feet in front of him.

Hyland removed a small flashlight from his pocket, shined it along the corridor, and limped through the debris toward the destruction. As he neared the damaged area, there were several large stones dislodged, but the structure remained intact. He stopped before a large pile of debris and shined his light across the area. His light shined on a bloody hand sticking out from beneath the rubble. He was able to locate the man's face.

One of his construction workers lay dead in the debris with a gun near his hand. Whether he'd been crushed or blown apart was irrelevant. As Hyland stared at the dead man and shook his head, a light was cast over him. He suddenly spun around with his rifle aimed in unison with his flashlight and prepared to shoot. A blue light shined through the haze and floating debris, lighting the entire corridor surrounding Hyland. A look of shock and possible horror swept over his face.

Chapter Forty-four

Regan, Leanne, Danika, and Tara were tied and gagged while sitting on the game room floor in the center of the room. Derek stood over them with his gun firmly in his hand. Anderson hid behind the partially open game room door while holding Regan's assault rifle.

"Regan, are you there?" came Jacklyn's voice over the nearby hand radio.

They looked at the radio on the coffee table. Tara slipped out of her ropes, removed her gag, and jumped up. Derek handed her the radio.

"Jacklyn, it's Tara. Where are you?" she gasped with a convincing sound of alarm in her tone. "Regan and Leanne were captured by Rick's men. I'm alone and really scared."

"Can you get to the south wing?" Jacklyn asked over the radio.

"I think so."

"There's a secret passageway through the conservatory," Jacklyn informed her through the radio. "You'll be safe there. We'll be there in ten minutes."

"Okay, I'm on my way," she replied then looked at her brother for instructions.

He nodded and removed his own radio. "I need everyone in the south wing conservatory," he announced into his radio. "Jacklyn's on her way."

Tara hurried from the room. Just on the other side of the wall behind the bookcase next to the fireplace, Jacklyn and Ellis hid in the bland secret passageway. Both looked through peek holes on opposite sides of the fireplace and observed the game room situation. Ellis looked from the peek hole to his watch then held his hand up to Jacklyn. She nodded she was ready.

Within the game room, Anderson stood by the door with the assault rifle while Derek paced by the fireplace. After Derek passed, the bookcase next to the fireplace opened with little sound. Anderson turned having heard something. Ellis stood within the secret passageway opening and shot Anderson. Derek turned with surprise on the other side of the fireplace and aimed his gun. A second passageway opened near him, striking him, and knocked him to the floor. Jacklyn jumped out, took his gun, and hurried for the others.

Ellis aimed his gun at Derek as he stood. "Flinch and I'll shoot."

Derek took the threat seriously and remained motionless with his hands in the air. The butler glided sideways to the main door, kicked the assault rifle away from the dead man, and peered out the partially open door into the hallway. Jacklyn quickly untied Regan. He then removed his gag and helped untie the others.

"They're probably backtracking after hearing the shots," Ellis informed them. "We don't have much time."

Jacklyn handed the ropes to Leanne and, with a nod of her head, indicated she should tie up Derek.

Leanne roughly tied Derek's hands behind his back. "Prick," she scoffed.

Derek sneered at her. Danika approached, smiled sweetly, and kicked him in the groin. He sank to his knees in agony.

"Now it's officially over," Danika snarled.

Leanne smiled and pulled Derek to his feet. Ellis tossed a gun to Regan and nodded to Derek. Regan took his cue and covered Derek.

"We need to get to the dock and warn Brandon," Jacklyn announced.

"You, Leanne, and Danika go to the dock, take care of Brandon's welcome party, and then sail to the mainland," Ellis informed them. "Regan and I will handle this."

Regan stared at him with surprise. "We will?"

Ellis looked into the hallway then eyed Regan. "It's clear. Let's go."

"Where, dude?"

"You're taking the trash to the study," Ellis informed him. "I'll see the ladies to the front door then join you."

§

The boat was already tied to the mostly destroyed dock. Brandon climbed down the rope ladder, removed his gun, and hurried for the beach. He no sooner entered the woods when he heard a gun cocking behind him forcing him to stop in his tracks. His gun was snatched from his hand. He held his hands in the air and turned to face Rick. Brandon showed little reaction.

"Hey, thanks for returning my boat," Rick announced cheerfully while grinning.

"Don't tell me you're the mastermind behind this," Brandon scoffed.

"Me? Nah, I'm just the mercenary for hire," Rick replied a little too cheerfully. "I believe you've met my squad--retired Special Forces."

Cooper stepped out of the tree line with an assault rifle cradled in his arms.

"Hyland never stood a chance against us," Rick announced with an amused laugh. "He's good, but he's not that good."

"My money's on the major," Brandon casually replied with little reaction. "He's probably mopping the dungeon floor with your boys as we speak."

"As much as I'd like to kill you, you're worth more alive if Jacklyn hasn't been caught yet," Rick announced then motioned him along the path.

Chapter Forty-five

Ellis, Jacklyn, Regan, Derek, Leanne, and Danika walked along the hallway in the direction of the foyer. Ellis nodded Regan and Derek to the study. The rest continued for the front door. The door opened to reveal Brandon. Jacklyn was relieved to see him then noted the look on his face. Jacklyn and Ellis immediately raised their guns. Rick and Cooper entered behind Brandon with their weapons aimed at the defenseless man.

"Put the weapons down," Rick snarled.

Regan pushed Derek into the hall with his gun aimed at his head while he partially hid in the doorway for protection.

"Like, you first, dude," Regan cried out.

Rick chuckled while eying the cook. "You'd never shoot an unarmed man, Regan."

Jacklyn took two steps back and aimed her gun at Derek's head. He immediately gasped with concern and eyed his man.

"She's serious, Rick," Derek cried out in genuine panic. "She also has twitchy fingers."

"It's true," Brandon casually remarked. "She once shot Ellis in the ass."

More guns were heard cocking behind Jacklyn and Derek. Ellis shut his eyes and groaned. Tara, Harry, and Norman stood in the hall behind them with their guns aimed.

"Very carefully lower that gun, Jacklyn," Harry snarled, "as if your life depended on it."

Jacklyn and Ellis lowered their guns. Regan dropped his gun from where he stood in the study doorway then darted inside the room and slammed the door, surprising everyone.

Harry approached Jacklyn and collected the weapons. "Will someone get doughboy out of there?"

Rick tossed Brandon into the hall. Jacklyn rushed into his arms and clung to him.

He held her and gave her a quick, sad kiss. "I'm sorry, Jacklyn. I'm not your uncle," he gently informed her. "I don't have multiple aces up my sleeve."

Cooper and Norman pounded on the study door with their weapons. "Come on out, Regan," Cooper ordered. "There's nowhere for you to go. Don't make us break it down."

Everyone seemed surprised when the study door opened a crack. A grenade rolled into the hall, and the door slammed shut. Cooper and Norman stared at the object and appeared horrified.

"Grenade!" Norman shouted.

Norman and Cooper leaped away from the grenade. Leanne and Danika screamed and dove to the floor. Brandon pushed Jacklyn against the wall to shield her, but she seemed more interested in reaching into his back pocket. Harry, Tara, and Derek turned to run. Ellis grabbed Harry's wrist and twisted his arm, forcing him to drop the gun. The grenade popped with a puff of smoke. Everyone except Ellis and Jacklyn reacted to the pop. Jacklyn spun out of Brandon's arms and flicked her wrist, extending Little Jimmy to three feet. Without hesitation, she struck Rick's arm, knocking the gun across the hall. She twirled the stick and struck him twice more in the face.

By the time the others realized the grenade was a dummy, Ellis was already spinning into a high, roundhouse kick, throwing Norman into the wall. As Cooper turned with his gun, Ellis spun into a series of kicks, knocking the gun from his hand with one and striking him in the face with the next. Cooper crashed into a nearby table. Norman removed a Bowie knife from his boot, rushed Ellis, and attempted to slash him. Ellis evaded the knife and swept Norman's legs out from under him. Tara was about to shoot Ellis when she heard a popping sound. Tara gasped, pulled a tiny dart from her neck, looked at it, and then sank to the floor. Regan stood in the study doorway with the dart gun.

Ellis deflected Norman's kicks and punches before Cooper joined in. Ellis fought both men without missing a beat. Jacklyn ran across the marble floor as Harry grabbed his discarded gun. She swung the stick as she slid across the floor on her hip and nailed Harry across the mid-section. He was thrown several feet. Derek dove for the discarded gun. Danika plowed into Derek, taking them both to the floor. As Rick moved to his feet, Brandon grabbed the discarded gun and aimed it at him. Rick kicked the gun from his hand and punched him in the face. When Brandon straightened, Rick grabbed the gun and casually shot him in the chest. Brandon gasped with surprise and struck the wall. Jacklyn turned to the sound of gunfire and watched in horror as Brandon collapsed to the floor.

"Brandon!"

Jacklyn attempted to run for Brandon but was held back by Regan. Rick grinned, stood over Brandon's motionless body, and raised his gun. Brandon painfully gasped and met Rick's sinister gaze. Rick noticed the strange, twisted smile on Brandon's face. He then saw the derringer hidden in Brandon's hand. Rick's smile suddenly faded as the derringer fired and shot him in the throat. Rick clutched his neck as he fell to the floor. Regan appeared surprised and released Jacklyn. She ran for Brandon and dropped to his side. He groaned while clutching his chest and attempted to sit up.

"Try not to move," she gasped.

Brandon sat up despite her plea. Jacklyn opened his shirt to reveal the bulletproof vest then met his gaze with a slightly surprised look.

He stared back at her and chuckled softly. "I'm glad the major is paranoid."

Danika screamed. Jacklyn looked back. Derek was on top of Danika and punched her in the face. Leanne screamed with anger and dove on Derek's back. Jacklyn ran for them. Brandon grabbed the discarded stick, rose more slowly, and hurried after her. Derek attempted to toss Leanne off him. Danika kicked Derek in the abdomen from her position on the floor. Derek was thrown backward and landed on top of Leanne, stunning her.

Ellis struck Norman in the face and knocked him to the floor. He turned just in time to block another kick from Cooper. Norman grabbed his discarded knife and stabbed Ellis in the thigh. Ellis cried out. Cooper struck him twice in the face, throwing him to the floor. Harry rejoined the fight after reclaiming his gun. Regan cried out while plowing into Harry, and tackled him into a suit of armor. Both men fell to the floor, and the gun flew from Harry's hand.

Cooper grabbed the gun as Jacklyn and Brandon approached and aimed it at Ellis, who was now on his knees attempting to stand despite the knife embedded in his thigh. Ellis looked up to see the gun aimed at his face. Danika cried out, jumped in front of Cooper while grabbing his wrist, and kept him from shooting Ellis in the head. The gun fired. Danika suddenly cried out in agony and fell to the floor. Cooper turned back to Ellis, who was now on his feet. As Cooper squeezed the trigger, Ellis knocked the gun from his hand, grabbed Cooper's head, and swiftly broke his neck in one fluid motion.

Brandon struck Norman with the stick, knocking the knife from his hand. Before he could swing again, Norman swept his legs out from under him. Norman jumped on Brandon and punched him. Regan punched Harry from their position on the floor in the scattered suit of armor. Harry got out from under the large cook and grabbed a discarded gun. Before he could even aim it at Regan, Jacklyn kicked Harry in the face and knocked him back several feet. A gun cocked near Jacklyn's head. She tensed to see Tara aiming the gun at her. This was becoming a habit. Norman punched Brandon once more and left him motionless on the floor then grabbed another gun and stood.

"Anyone moves and Jacklyn gets it," Tara suddenly cried out.

Leanne painfully touched her head while half sitting on the floor on the opposite end of the hall from Regan. Regan turned onto his back by the destroyed suit of armor and stared at the unfolding scene. Brandon remained lying motionless on the floor near the stairs. Ellis scanned the room while Derek and Harry collected weapons.

"Get some rope to tie them up," Harry said to Derek. "We'll lock them in the dungeon. That will be the end of their interference."

Norman aimed his gun at Ellis' head, his finger tight on the trigger, and appeared unstable. "We should kill them," he snarled in anger.

"They're as good as dead in the dungeon," Harry announced firmly.

Tara hit Jacklyn on the back of the head with the gun. She collapsed to the floor near Brandon. Ellis flinched and stared at the gun pointed at his face.

"Just tie them up," Harry again ordered.

Norman removed the gun from Ellis' face with disgust. Jacklyn slid alongside Brandon despite her moderate disorientation. She pulled his head onto her lap and gently stroked his battered and bleeding face.

"Brandon?" she whispered.

With blood streaking his face, Brandon opened his eyes and looked at Jacklyn. He gave her an odd, tiny smile and shut his eyes.

"I'm really turned on right now."

Jacklyn appeared baffled then tensed at what he'd just said. She eyed Ellis, who now stared at her with concern. Derek hurried down the hall for the game room to gather the rope when he suddenly stopped and dropped his gun. The clatter of the gun hitting the floor alerted everyone. They looked at Derek as he slowly backed away from the game room with his hands raised. Hyland, covered in debris and dried blood, limped into the hallway from the game room with a gun aimed at Derek's forehead and a slightly psychotic, twisted smile on his face.

"What's this? A party?" he asked almost cheerfully. "Now why wasn't I invited?"

"Uncle Hyland--?" Derek gasped.

His smile twisted into a sneer. "I'm not your uncle," Hyland snarled. "You're just a walking dead man. Understand?"

Derek appeared terrified and managed a tiny nod. Hyland eyed everyone in the hallway, assessing the situation, which didn't look good. Harry kept his gun aimed at Jacklyn from where he stood near Brandon's feet. Norman again had his gun aimed at Ellis' face. Hyland maintained his twisted, evil smile, despite the guns aimed at Jacklyn and Ellis.

"Well, ain't this a pretty sight?" Hyland announced then eyed Ellis, grinning his pleasure. "Nice to see you've still got that magical touch, Captain."

"Like riding a bike, Major," Ellis casually replied despite his situation.

Their exchange was enough to strike Harry with concern. It was the first anyone knew Ellis had been under Hyland's command during his stint in the military.

"Enough talk, Hyland," Harry announced boldly. "You're going to release Derek and throw your gun down, or I kill Jacklyn. It's that simple."

Hyland suddenly laughed, chilling everyone. "Nothing's ever that simple, Harry. For example--" His smile suddenly faded as he shouted, "--you killing my sister, my best friend, and my wife, you son-of-a-bitch!" Hyland collected his anger and again resumed his twisted smile. "But I'm a reasonable man. I might be willing to let you live with most of your body parts intact. However--" he announced as his eyes suddenly narrowed. "--*he's* not as forgiving."

Hyland indicated the foyer on the other end of the hall from him. Everyone looked toward the foyer and the front door. Simon stood in the foyer with blood streaking his face. His clothes were tattered, slightly singed, and still damp. Jacklyn gasped with horror while staring at her friend. An unarmed Simon stared at Harry with a frozen, psychotic look. His hand subconsciously twitched at his side.

Harry laughed at the unfolding scene then looked back at Hyland. "Am I supposed to be scared?" he demanded with humor. "He's not even armed."

Jacklyn stared at Harry, who shifted his attention between Hyland and Simon on opposite sides of the hallway. She slowly slid her hand along Brandon's waist and silently opened his belt. Ellis' eyes shifted from Jacklyn to Norman and the gun in his face. Regan's eyes shifted from Jacklyn to Leanne, who sat across the hall from him. Her hand was on the dart gun beneath her thigh. Leanne met Regan's gaze in silent suggestion. He gave a tiny nod.

Hyland maintained his psychotic grin while staring at Simon. "Are they here?"

"Awaiting your orders, Major," Simon growled while showing little emotion.

Hyland suddenly chuckled, sending chills through everyone. "Fire at will."

Simon's look remained fixated and angered. The front doors suddenly flew open, and a violent gust of wind blew past Simon and into the hall, startling everyone. Hyland maintained his twisted smile and didn't flinch. Every door in the hall slammed shut one after another with thunderous cracks. Everyone looked around with surprise as the wind continued to blow. Everyone except Jacklyn. She swiftly opened Brandon's pants.

Ellis looked from the blowing wind to Jacklyn then cast a look at Leanne. Leanne slid the dart gun across the floor to Regan. Regan caught it under his hand and immediately hid it. A heavy gust of wind flew down the grand staircase with what appeared to be glowing ghostly images traveling within it. Shrill cries were heard as they passed. A ghostly image appeared before Harry's face. Lady Brighton's ghost stared into his eyes with hatred. Her ghostly hands grabbed him by the throat as she screamed in his face.

"No, it can't be!" Harry cried out with terror, aimed his gun at her, and fired several shots.

The bullets passed through her and nearly struck his men. Derek ran from Hyland, who remained humored while watching the scene unfold. The ghosts circled the room in a small tornado. Objects rattled and doors slammed throughout the mansion. Ellis took advantage of the situation and knocked the gun from Norman's hand then kicked him backward. Regan removed the dart gun and shot Tara in the buttocks. She gasped while removing the dart, stared at it, and then collapsed to the floor. Derek ran past the action as ghosts dive-bombed him while he screamed. Danika grabbed his ankle and took him to the floor with her despite her bleeding shoulder. She half lay on him and glared into his eyes.

"Where do you think you're going, you bastard," she cried out in anger.

Derek kicked her in the abdomen, scrambled to his feet, and ran for Simon and the front door. Norman kicked Ellis, tossing him backward then lunged for him. Ellis threw himself to the floor, yanked the knife from his own thigh as he rolled, and threw it at Norman, striking him in the neck. Norman clutched the knife in his throat, spit up blood, and collapsed. Harry saw the ambush unfolding and aimed his gun at Jacklyn, his only ace in the hole.

To his surprise, Jacklyn's hand was down Brandon's pants to his thigh. The gun from Brandon's hidden thigh holster fired as the bullet ripped through his pants and hit Harry in the chest. Harry clutched his bleeding chest then looked at the barrel of the gun sticking out of Brandon's pants. Harry gasped and collapsed. Derek ran for Simon and the open front door. Simon spun into a roundhouse kick and struck Derek in the face. He flew backward with force and struck the floor. Simon casually straightened. Jacklyn clung to Brandon, who continued to breathe harshly from her thigh shot.

She smiled slyly at Simon. "Nice kick."

"I had a good teacher," he teased.

Jacklyn laughed in response. Regan and Leanne scrambled to their feet and tended to Danika, who sat up while clutching her bleeding shoulder. Ellis kneeled alongside her while holding his own bleeding thigh. He checked her wound and offered a warm smile.

"You're going to be okay, Danika," Ellis announced then looked at Regan next to him. "Get my field kit from the study."

Regan nodded and hurried to the study. Simon and Hyland approached Jacklyn, who still held Brandon. Despite his injured leg, Hyland crouched near them and shook his head at Brandon.

"How long do you intend to milk the sympathy?" Hyland demanded.

"Hey, while you were off playing hide-and-seek in the dungeon, I was being shot, beaten, and had a gun fired just inches from my boys," Brandon announced. "I'm entitled to a little sympathy."

Brandon took Jacklyn's arm, secured it over his chest, and glared at Hyland. Hyland laughed, smacked Brandon on the thigh, and straightened. Simon kneeled near Jacklyn. Jacklyn released Brandon, who nearly hit the floor, and hugged Simon. He returned the embrace.

Brandon frowned and slowly sat up. "So ends my sympathy."

"I thought you were dead," Jacklyn gasped while almost down to tears.

"Thankfully, I had a guardian angel watching over me," Simon announced then nodded over his shoulder.

Jacklyn looked past him and saw her Aunt Mara's ghost. She slowly stood and approached the smiling ghost. Jacklyn returned the smile and reached out her hand. She touched Jacklyn's hand. Hyland watched with tears in his eyes. Jacklyn looked at Hyland, smiled at Mara, and then walked away. Hyland approached Mara and smiled as tears streaked his face.

"Do you have to go?" Hyland asked.

"Yes, darling," Lady Brighton replied.

Hyland moved closer to her, placed his hands on her ghostly face, and gently kissed her. She returned the kiss. Hyland released her, wiped his eyes, and quickly limped away. Ellis looked at the ghostly woman from his position on the floor. They exchanged knowing smiles.

"You *are* the storm, Captain," Mara announced with humor then suddenly vanished.

Hyland entered his study and shut the door behind him, wanting to be alone with his grief. Brandon moved to his feet and clung to Jacklyn.

Jacklyn eyed him and grinned. "You were pretty amazing; you know that?"

"I got myself captured, shot, and beaten," Brandon announced. "Not exactly impressive."

"You shielded me from what you thought was a grenade, stood up to a trained killer, and went after a man with a knife," Jacklyn informed him. "But most importantly, you trusted me to shoot a gun strapped not three inches from a very important part of your body. I love you for that, and I've never been so turned on in my life."

Brandon groaned and kissed her warmly but passionately. He then pulled away and looked into her eyes with a tiny smile.

"You don't know how badly I want to act on that," he announced then grimaced, "but when that gun fired, important parts evacuated the scene."

She laughed softly. "I'd be more than happy to help you find them later."

Brandon held her in his arms and groaned softly. "I'll take you up on that offer."

Chapter Forty-six

The following evening, Regan removed a tray of cookies from the oven and set them on the counter. Hyland and Ellis limped into the kitchen with haggard expressions on their weary faces.

"I don't remember gunshots hurting this much before," Hyland remarked.

"It's been years since we've abused our bodies like this, Major," Ellis replied with a sigh.

"Yeah," Hyland announced then grinned deviously. "I miss those days."

"I prefer being able to stand without someone helping me," Ellis muttered.

Hyland sat at the counter with discomfort and glared at Regan. "I told you to take a few days off."

"People still have to eat, and I like cookies," Regan informed him. "Besides, like, baking relaxes me." He cast a glance at Ellis. "How's our other patient?"

"Danika's resting comfortably," Ellis replied.

"That was nice of you to insist she stay here rather than a hospital, although I'm surprised she agreed," Regan remarked.

"Considering what you were up against, I'm proud none of you ended up in body bags," Hyland announced.

"What we were up against?" Ellis asked.

"Younger versions of us," Hyland teased.

Jacklyn, Leanne, and Danika appeared from the back stairs and entered the kitchen. Ellis appeared concerned and limped toward them.

"You should be upstairs resting," he informed Danika.

"I'm fine, though I won't be dancing anytime soon," she replied and giggled.

Hyland and Regan eyed each other and hid their smiles. Danika joined Hyland at the table. Ellis approached Danika and appeared upset with her.

"What you did yesterday was very stupid," Ellis informed her with genuine anger.

Hyland slid off his stool and limped from the kitchen. Jacklyn and Leanne pulled Regan from the kitchen after Hyland.

Danika glanced at Ellis and offered a tiny smile. "You're welcome."

"No, it doesn't work that way," Ellis informed her. "You put yourself between a trained killer and me, and it almost got you killed."

Danika casually shrugged. "So you owe me one."

"I owe you one?"

She slipped off her stool, walked behind the counter, and removed a cookie from the baking sheet.

Ellis glared at her. "If you had died taking a bullet meant for me--"

"Honestly, I'd think you'd be a little more appreciative," Danika announced. "If you had saved my life, we'd be getting drunk and having wild sex right about now. So, really, where's your appreciation?"

Chapter Forty-seven

Hyland, Regan, and Jacklyn sat at the game room bar with drinks before them. Hyland looked at Leanne, who massaged Simon's shoulders and whispered in his ear. Both laughed softly at whatever she'd said.

Hyland looked back at his drink. "I guess ghost boy is getting lucky tonight," he muttered into his glass, took a sip, and then looked at Jacklyn. "Speaking of the young and horny, where's Brandon? I haven't seen him since the police left."

"I think I scared him impotent," she muttered.

"Dude, you shot a gun off three inches from his manhood," Regan announced while staring at her. "I'm scared just sitting next to you."

"Thinking about it," Hyland remarked. "I'm even afraid to sit next to you."

"Thanks for cheering me up."

Simon stood, placed his arm around Leanne, and guided her from the game room. All three watched them leave, frowned, and returned to their drinks. Brandon entered and placed his hand on Regan's shoulder.

"I just came from the kitchen. You'll want to throw out those cookies," Brandon gently informed him then muttered, "and consider replacing the countertop."

"Dude!" he exclaimed. "They're going at it on the counter?"

Regan groaned and poured another drink. Hyland frowned and extended his glass. Jacklyn extended hers as well.

Brandon eyed the three then glared at Jacklyn. "Okay, I get the major and Regan indulging in a pity party, but what's dragging you down with them?"

"I broke you," she muttered. "Even my tough as nails uncle fears for his manhood sitting next to me."

Hyland chuckled into his glass.

Brandon took the glass from her. "I think you've had enough." He glared at Regan and Hyland. "Thanks for getting her drunk for me."

"Anytime, dude."

Brandon led Jacklyn from the game room.

Brandon guided Jacklyn along the dimly lit north wing corridor. She looked around the moderately dark and creepy area then gave him a curious look.

"What are we doing here?"

"I wanted to surprise you," Brandon announced then opened the ballroom door.

Jacklyn and Brandon entered the ballroom. The entire room was cleaned to a breathtaking, almost restored condition. The marble floor was polished, the ceiling was free of cobwebs, and the chandeliers sparkled. The large windows with stained glass glistened in the candlelight from hundreds of candles, lending a romantic atmosphere. A neatly made mattress was on the floor along with a bottle of champagne.

"You did all this?"

"Well, Simon helped."

Brandon pressed play on the CD player positioned on the polished grand piano. Slow, romantic piano music played. Brandon smiled and extended his hand to her. She accepted his hand, and they danced across the ballroom. As they danced the waltz, glowing ghostly images danced with them filling the room with laughter.

The End

Other books by Holly Copella!
Reviews left on Amazon are appreciated!

"The Battle for Andrea María"

A cruise ship attack turns six survivors into overnight celebrities after they take credit for the heroic act of a stowaway who died saving them.

The cruise is just what Jess needed--a bit of harmless fun far from her daily grind. But what begins as a relaxing vacation turns into a desperate fight for her life when terrorists take over the ship and start piling up bodies. Teaming up with a mysterious stowaway, Jess attempts to send out a distress call but knows they cannot wait for help to come. If she or the few remaining passengers have any hope for survival, Jess must act now. The papers dub it "The Battle for *Andrea Maria*," but to Jess it is the moment she fought side-by-side with her enigmatic Romeo, saving the ship--and losing him. She thinks the story ends there, but really, the nightmare is just beginning...

"Insanely Deadly"

When the dead return to life, it's up to an admiral's daughter and a mildly insane, former war hero to save their small town.

Jetta Cross, a Navy Admiral's daughter, is tasked with keeping her father's comrade, a former war hero turned town crazy, grounded in the real world. Capt. John Hunter is still fighting the war in his head, where imaginary dead people are part of his world. When a viral outbreak brings about a zombie uprising, Hunter is left to his own devices. He must resume his role as a one-man commando unit in order to destroy the ravenous undead. With Hunter still fighting his own inner demons as well as the undead, the townspeople fear their zombie neighbors may not be the only threat. Stranded at the island's luxurious resort with a handful of workers, Jetta is forced to live up to her father's reputation and take charge of the deteriorating situation at the hotel. She must wage her own war against the infected before the government declares her hometown a total loss.

"Deadly Institution"

A town recluse suspected of killing his wife teams up with a young woman in order to stop a killer.

After being accused of murdering his wife, Konrad Asher turns his back on the town that once adored him. Ten years later, he still holds his grudge and the title of the most feared man in town. With the reopening of the burned mental institution, where his wife had died, former employees are now murdered one-by-one, throwing suspicion back on Asher. A young local reporter, Jacey, is forced to reveal her long-time friendship with the infamous recluse in order to clear his name not only in the recent murders but to exonerate him in the death of his wife as well. Will Jacey's relationship with Asher invite the killer closer to her? Or is the killer already in her life?

"Screenplays: The Island Collection"
"Jungle Princess", "A.L.F. Resort", "Brighton Island"

Discover how romance and fun in the sun can be downright *chilling*!

"Jungle Princess" is a romantic/thriller that leaves a teenage girl stranded on an island with two male shipmates and a creature of "unknown" origin. She soon discovers the island is home to an abandoned prison with several prisoners roaming free. What really killed over one hundred prisoners? And is it still out there--?

"A.L.F. Resort" is a romantic/thriller set on an island resort with Artificial Life Forms as the main draw. At this resort, all your fantasies come true...until a malfunction removes safety inhibitors on the A.L.F.'s. Zombies, biker gangs, and mobsters run amuck, turning fantasies into nightmares. A young reporter gets more of a story than she anticipates, but will she survive long enough to write the story?

"Brighton Island" is a romantic/thriller set on a private island. When the owner's niece brings her psychic friend to the mansion, his presence awakens the spirits' tortured souls. As the psychic attempts to solve the old murders, the niece is confronted with the possibility that she's next to join the mansion ghosts. Stranded on the island with a crazed killer, her uncle wages his own war to save them. Will his "shock and awe" tactics actually save them or get them killed?

"Death Displacement"

A grief-stricken man travels back in time to seek revenge on the woman who murdered his girlfriend but inadvertently falls in love with her.

Kane is about to marry the woman he loves. His life is perfect. A few weeks before the wedding, a vindictive woman from his girlfriend's past mysteriously arrives and kills her. He learns of a traumatic accident that happened five years earlier, which triggers Riley's hatred for his girlfriend. Distraught over his girlfriend's death, Kane uses an antique time machine to travel into the past in order to find and destroy the woman responsible. When he runs into Riley's younger self, he realizes she's not the monster she later becomes, and he can't bring himself to destroy her. With a little help from his oddball friend from the past, they formulate a plan to prevent the accident that sends Riley down her destructive path. Kane's plan backfires when he falls for the younger Riley. His new tortured existence is further complicated when future Riley, his girlfriend's killer, shows up with her own devious agenda that doesn't include him. Will he be able to stop the time ripple, which ultimately ends with his girlfriend's death? Or will future Riley take him out of the timeline forever--

"Dead Village"

After strange happenings isolate a small resort town from the rest of the world, nearly one hundred residents seek refuge at the closed hotel. Only eight survive the night. And that's just the beginning...

One day after the entire population of Fox Ridge Village disappears, a car wreck forces several unsuspecting crash victims to seek help at the closed summer hotel. Within the hotel, they discover the grisly aftermath of a brutal slaughter. Crash victims Vander and Devon, a reluctant clairvoyant, team up to solve the riddle of the "haunted hotel" and the mass hysteria plaguing the remaining survivors. By the time they discover the hotel's secret, they're already drawn into the hysteria. As the body count continues to climb, it's a race to isolate the source and bring everyone back to reality before they kill one another. Will Devon be able to communicate with the traumatized spirits before their fate becomes her own?

"Misfits, Inc."

A seemingly ordinary, young woman meets four misfits who claim she has given them supernatural powers.

While on a business trip to a remote island paradise, a bored secretary, Hailey, has her world turned upside down when her path collides with a psychic freak, Skyler. He attempts to convince her that they had met in his dreams, and she had chosen him as one of her four mystic warriors. After Skyler foresees a woman's death, they discover an unidentified creature has killed one of the guests. They are joined by a lounge pianist and a rich playboy, who also claim they had met her in their dreams. If Skyler's prophecies are genuine, the evil entity controlling the ravenous creatures needs to destroy Hailey to ensure its survival. Reluctantly accepting her fate, Hailey has to locate the last and most powerful of her chosen warriors, The Guardian. Their fate is in doubt when The Guardian turns out to be a self-absorbed, former cat burglar with a bad attitude. Can Hailey turn her company of misfits into an elite team of mystic warriors? Or will The Guardian's secret agenda destroy them all?

"Basement Dwellers"

A viral outbreak at a hospital leaves a mortician, sheriff, and coroner fighting for their lives against a horde of undead and the CDC.

After a massive car wreck leaves several survivors in critical condition at the local hospital, a surgeon uses experimental drugs on his critical patients and accidentally causes a zombie outbreak. When local mortician, Lexx, receives an infected corpse as her client, she becomes stranded in the hospital basement during CDC quarantine along with the local sheriff and the coroner. The infamous surgeon struggles to find a cure for his infectious blunder by using the other survivors as test subjects. Meanwhile, Lexx and the sheriff attempt to locate his missing sister, who's stranded somewhere in the battle zone that once was the emergency room. It's a race against time and the ravenous undead. Can they survive the undead before CDC sanitizes the hospital of all infection?

"Witness Protection"
Also available in audiobook!

After witnessing an execution, a resourceful young woman attempts to disappear while being pursued by a hitman and a handsome federal agent.

A helicopter pilot, Jackie Remus, reluctantly agrees to go on a date with one of her clients, but her date is unexpectedly cut short when she witnesses a man being murdered. After narrowly escaping with her life, she is placed into protective custody. When the safe house is breached, Jackie makes a daring escape from both the hired killers and the handsome FBI agent, who wants to return her to protective custody. With a little help from her sly and crafty friend, Monroe, Jackie is convinced she can disappear until the trial. While on her journey to meet with her friend, she solicits help from a few shady but lovable characters along the way. Although she manages to stay one-step ahead of the hired killers, the federal agent remains in hot pursuit. Will Jackie reach Monroe before she's captured by the FBI and returned to protective custody? Or will the hired killers silence her first?

"Town Darling"

After surviving a brutal attack that claims the lives of those she loves, a young woman seeks revenge on a corrupt town.

Going back home is never easy, but for Casey, it means returning to her corrupt hometown where she barely survived a brutal attack. Accompanied by two family friends, she seeks justice for the night that destroyed her life. Her physical scars are nothing compared to her emotional ones, forcing the local sheriff to believe that the town darling is back for revenge. As the conspiracy for her revenge appears to be leading up to the coveted town fair, the sheriff is determined to stop her from fulfilling her vengeful scheme...but guilt over his role on that fateful night continues to haunt him. Will his desperate need for Casey's forgiveness be his undoing? Or will Casey's desire for revenge destroy them both?

"Unconditional"

A young woman puts her life on hold to care for an unstable, highly skilled combat soldier, who believes someone is trying to kill him.

A botched military coup leaves a team of elite fighters injured with one clinging to life in a coma. When Harlan wakes from his coma, he's left with no memory of his past life. His commander's daughter, Indy, takes it upon herself to care for the fallen war hero. She's challenged with more than just his physical care as she combats with not only his memory loss but also his newly found desire for her. His infatuation with her becomes the least of her worries when he sinks back into his role of a combat soldier. Believing his life is in danger, his fighting skills surface, turning him into an unpredictable and dangerous man. Will his memory return to him before Indy is forced to commit him? Or will he finally find his nemesis, "the coyote", and possibly claim the life of an innocent person?

"Witness Protection 2"
The Return of Whiskey Tango Foxtrot

Believing she holds the clue to millions in missing laundered money, a young woman is placed into the protective care of a former Navy SEAL team.

Feeling sorry for her recently separated co-worker, Leeann invites Wiley to join her and her friends on their night out. Little does she know that finding her co-worker murdered is just the beginning of her nightmare. Leeann unknowingly holds the key to fifty million dollars in potentially laundered mob money. With hired killers pursuing her, the FBI places her into a different kind of protective custody. Former Navy SEAL team Whiskey Tango Foxtrot reunites to keep Leeann alive at their secret hideaway. What should be an easy assignment takes an unscheduled turn when secrets, lies, and betrayal threaten to derail their mission. Is the team prepared for a war on their own doorstep? Will Leeann's misguided trust endanger the lives of those sent to protect her?

"Deadly Institution 2"

When blackmail turns into murder, a young woman finds herself caught in the killer's crosshairs.

The small town of Stony Ridge is no stranger to scandal and persecution of the innocent. When a brutal killing shakes the town's prestigious country club, Jacey McMurray seeks help from a self-proclaimed vigilante, Konrad Asher. As her professional and personal worlds collide, Jacey fears the stress of the country club killings have finally taken their toll on Asher. Can a stressed out vigilante stop the killer before he strikes again?

"Witness Protection 3"
Alpha Mike Foxtrot

A helicopter pilot risks her life to help a team of retired Navy SEALs rescue two girls from a killer.

When former Navy SEAL team Whiskey Tango Foxtrot asks for a simple favor, Jackie reluctantly offers her air-taxi services. What could go wrong? What begins as a search and rescue for two girls turns into a fight for survival against a heavily armed drug cartel. Wanted by the law with the cartel in hot pursuit and their home base breached, the team is forced to call in a favor from a questionable ally. Unfortunately, their new safe house isn't what it seems. Without knowing who the real enemy is, can Jackie and the team save their young witnesses from the hands of a killer?

"The Pen Pal"

In order to save her friend, she must enter the mind of a serial killer.

When her best friend is abducted, no one believes Jolynn saw it in a psychic vision. With nowhere to turn, Jolynn reluctantly joins Agent Harris Slade and his team on their hunt for a sadistic serial killer known only as "The Pen Pal". Finally confronted with the killer, Jolynn realizes she must enter the mind of the psychopath in order to stop the brutal killings. But when her vision reveals a particularly disturbing death, can Jolynn sacrifice her lover for her friend?

"Awaken the Dead"

A grieving innkeeper struggles to keep her haunted hotel out of foreclosure.

After losing her parents in a suspicious boating accident, Harley Brandon is determined to keep the family hotel out of foreclosure. Unfortunately, the hotel ghosts have other plans. Built with tainted money, the century old Horizon Hotel thrives on a tradition of murder, scandal, and suicide. As the paranormal activity increases to alarming levels, Harley discovers the truth about the hotel and its residents. Can Harley save her friends from the hotel's frightening hidden secrets?

"Already Dead"
Supernatural Collection

From the already dead to the undead. Three supernatural tales of "things that go bump in the night".

"Bloodletting" - A vampire themed resort allows guests to *participate* in their Bloodletting Ritual to celebrate the island's legendary vampires.

"Reaper of Souls" - A young woman must outwit an evil sorcerer in order to save her brother or become one of his minions forever.

"Already Dead" - When Flight 220 crashes, ten passengers make it to an isolated island, but only one man lives to tell the lie.

"Witness Protection 4"
O-Dark-Hundred

A simple assignment turns deadly when a retired Navy SEAL team uncovers a plot to kill a notorious mob boss.

When Whiskey Tango Foxtrot embarks on a simple stalking case, they're not prepared for a trip to a private island paradise owned by an infamous mobster. With one of their own suffering from traumatic head injuries, the team is left scrambling to decide what is real or imagined. The situation escalates even further when they uncover an assassination plot where everyone is a suspect. Now targets themselves, can the team survive their trip to paradise?

"Witness Protection 5"
Outside the Wire

After suffering several casualties on their last assignment, a retired Navy SEAL team discovers their misery is just beginning.

When Whiskey Tango Foxtrot returns home after suffering a devastating loss, they're hit with even more bad news regarding the rest of their team. Their grief is cut short when they discover their names are all on the same hit list. Hunted by relentless assassins, the scattered team must decide whether to remain safely hidden or find the man who put the price on their heads. Against the wishes of her teammates, Jackie strikes out on her own in order to save a friend who wants her dead. In a kill or be killed situation, will Jackie's emotions finally betray her?

"Once Upon a Disaster"

A young homicide detective finds herself at the mercy of a hitman in the aftermath of an earthquake

While investigating the murder of a hitman, Detective Jade Wesson pursues a lead connecting the dead man to a break-in at a computer programming company. She's drawn into the world of nightclub owner and front man for the mob, Cody Riley. Her investigation keeps pointing to Cody's right-hand man and possible hitman, Vahn Lott. Despite her efforts to keep her investigation on track, Vahn has plans of his own for the attractive detective. When an unprecedented earthquake rocks their east coast town, Jade must put her life in Vahn's hands if she wants to survive. Can she trust a man who might be the killer she's hunting?

"The Murder of Emily Fisher"

After finding their favorite teacher murdered, the lives of two teenage girls are forever changed.

Everyone loved Emily Fisher. While walking home one afternoon, two teenage girls, Sidney and Trisha, stumble upon a gruesome murder scene. The brutal murder of Emily Fisher, a young, attractive schoolteacher, shocks the small town of **Marilina**. After graduation, Sidney moves far away from the memories of the small town while Trisha retreats deeper into denial. Eight years after the murder, Sidney receives a desperate call from her childhood friend, forcing her to return home. Trisha believes Emily's killer was falsely accused and she manages to turn the entire town against her while attempting to prove it. When Trisha receives a death threat, Sidney realizes there may be some credibility to her friend's wild accusations. Is Trisha's mental breakdown a result of childhood trauma? Or is the real killer actually attempting to silence her? In order to save her friend, Sidney must answer the eight-year-old question. Who murdered Emily Fisher?

"Castle Bloodshed"
Murder Collection"

From a deadly island paradise to haunted castles. Three novella length tales of murder, mystery, and malicious intent.

"Castle Bloodshed" – A tour of Wesley Castle turns into a fight for survival as six stranded tourists discover the haunting secrets within the castle walls. A mystery writer teams up with an uptight butler in order stop a killer who may already be dead. Novella length paranormal murder mystery.

"Fleshies" – Is Uncle Rutger crazy? Five years ago, four business partners died within their newly purchased, fixer-upper castle. Their bodies were never found. The surviving partner, Rutger, claims a demon keeps him as its slave. Rutger's nephew schemes to save his uncle by sacrificing the lives of a group of stranded motorists and a high-profile novelist. Novella length supernatural murder mystery.

"Demon Island" – A group of strangers are invited to a remote island for the reading of a will. The guests soon discover they were brought to the island to be executed one-by-one. It's up to a private detective and a tenacious young woman to solve the murders and find a way to escape paradise. Novella length murder mystery.

Coming Soon!
"Witness Protection 6"

ABOUT THE AUTHOR

Holly Copella has been writing since the age of twelve when her frustration at a book's poor plot drove her to author her own story. Over the last decade, she's written a number of screenplays, some of which she's now adapting into novels. Her fascination with zombies and other darker material lends an edge to her writing, which tends to lean toward horror. As a fan of Agatha Christie, she appreciates the craft of a good plot and the importance of creating significant characters.

Hailing from Pennsylvania, Copella lives in the Endless Mountains on a farm with her rescue horses and other animals. In addition to writing and reading fiction, she enjoys riding horses and traveling to Las Vegas and Disney World.

www.ingramcontent.com/pod-product-compliance
Lightning Source LLC
Chambersburg PA
CBHW061158170626
46809CB00003B/1151